Jenny Oldfield

DOLPHIN ISLAND

Survival

Illustrations by
Daniel Howarth

Hodder
Children's
Books

For lovely Lola, Jude and Evan – three dedicated dolphin fans

HODDER CHILDREN'S BOOKS

First published in Great Britain in 2018 by Hodder and Stoughton

1 3 5 7 9 10 8 6 4 2

Text copyright © Jenny Oldfield, 2018

Inside illustrations copyright © Daniel Howarth, 2018

The moral rights of the author and illustrator have been asserted.

A CIP catalogue record for this book is available from the British Library.

ISBN 978 1 444 92829 7

Typeset in ITC Caslon 224

Printed and bound in Great Britain by Clays Ltd, St Ives plc

The paper and board used in this book are made from wood
from responsible sources.

Hodder Children's Books
An imprint of Hachette Children's Group
Part of Hodder and Stoughton
Carmelite House
50 Victoria Embankment
London EC4Y 0DZ

An Hachette UK Company
www.hachette.co.uk

www.hachettechildrens.co.uk

Chapter One

'I can see a ship!' Mia cried. She pointed to the horizon. 'Ship! Ship!'

From their lookout ledge high on the rugged hill, Fleur and Alfie strained to see.

'Where?' Fleur demanded. The blue sea sparkled; the sinking sun gradually turned the sky pink.

'There!' Mia jumped up and down as she waved and pointed. 'Help!' she yelled at the distant container ship. 'We're stuck on Dolphin Island. Come and rescue us … please!'

'They won't hear you,' Fleur muttered. Ah yes, she saw it – a faraway ship, so small she couldn't make out any details. It was the first they'd spotted for days. 'Hurry – let's put more wood on the fire. Maybe they'll see the smoke.'

Alfie lugged two heavy branches along the ledge and flung them on the fire. Sparks flew and flames licked at the wood. Smoke rose high into the clear sky.

'This way – look over here!' Mia cried.

The ship sailed steadily from east to west, crawling along the horizon with its heavy cargo.

'Please! ...' Mia held her breath and watched it sail on without altering course. '... It's not coming,' she whimpered at last.

The sun sank further in the west and smoke billowed from their fire into their eyes.

'What's up? Why are you crying?' Alfie flung the gruff questions at Fleur as he threw a final log into the flames.

'I'm not. It's the smoke,' she sniffed. The sailors hadn't seen their signal. Hope of rescue faded with the dying light.

'Why didn't they see us?' Mia wanted to know. Her dirty cheeks were streaked with what were definitely tears.

'It was too far away,' Fleur explained. She tried to cover her disappointment for Mia's sake. 'Don't worry

– someone will come looking for us before too long. We won't have to stay here for ever.'

'It only feels like for ever,' Alfie grumbled.

It was Day 17 on Dolphin Island – two and a half long weeks since the storm had driven their boat *Merlin* on to the rocks and cast the family into the sea. They'd all made it to the shore – Alfie, plus his younger sister, Mia, then Fleur, the oldest of the three kids, and their mum and dad. Their dad, James, was injured but everyone was safe. They'd built a camp and two fires, found fresh water, foraged and fished and found a way to survive.

'Hang on a second.' Mia rubbed the tears from her eyes and began to point once more. 'I can see something.'

Alfie and Fleur sighed and shook their heads.

'No, look!' There was movement far out to sea. Half a dozen curved fins cut rapidly through the water. A sleek grey shape leaped clear of the waves, then another and another. Others joined them and the creatures arced through the air then disappeared with a splash of their mighty tails.

'Oh, wow – cool!' Alfie breathed.

Dolphins! Not just any dolphins, but their special pod – all swimming swiftly in the white wake of the gigantic ship, rushing to catch up and attract the attention of the men on board.

'Go, Jazz! Go, Stormy! Go, Pearl!' Fleur yelled.

The three kids held their breaths again and watched as the dolphins sped alongside the ship, tiny from this distance and impossible to make out who was who. They breached the water and twisted and rolled in midair, disappeared under the frothing, foaming waves then came up to the surface again. They surged ahead and circled around the bow wave made by the enormous vessel as it cut through the clear turquoise water.

'Oh – don't get too close!' Fleur was worried for Jazz and the others. The ship was as big as a block of flats, casting an enormous shadow, powering on.

'I think they're trying to steer the ship around, to make them notice our fire.' Alfie was the one who figured it out. He'd read in a book about marine mammals that dolphins were smart and brave enough to help in this way. 'More branches!' he muttered as he fed the flames on their ledge at Lookout Point.

'Too close!' Fleur groaned. She put a hand over her eyes, unable to look.

The dolphins swam in formation ahead of the ship, by now an indistinct black block silhouetted against a crimson sun. They did everything they could to make it turn around.

'It's not working,' Mia wailed. The ship ignored the dolphins and sailed on.

'No, it's not,' Alfie agreed, looking anxiously for their pod of friendly dolphins after they disappeared from view. He spotted them swimming away from the container vessel, heading straight towards the island. 'It's OK, Fleur – you can look now.'

She peered through her fingers at their very own dolphins – Jazz, Pearl and Stormy – approaching the shore, leaving behind the rest of their pod, who rested by the reef where *Merlin* had finally gone down. 'Let's go and meet them,' she told Mia and Alfie.

She was first off the ledge and down the steep, rocky slope towards the waterfall where Alfie overtook her and went ahead down the cliff path on to the beach. They both stopped by the palm trees to catch their breath, giving Mia a chance to scamper ahead, across the white sand to the water's edge.

Six-year-old Mia ran into the breaking waves. She was dressed in shorts and T-shirt, wearing her home-made straw hat with its bright red and yellow feathers poking straight up from the brim.

'Watch out for your hat!' Fleur called as Mia plunged headlong.

Too late – the hat came off and bobbed in the waves.

'Stormy!' Mia greeted her cheeky, adventurous, dark grey friend. He opened his beak and chattered a reply – a series of creaks and clicks as he let her fling her arms around him.

'Thank heavens, you're safe,' Fleur told Jazz as she ran into the water and he gave her his high-low, high-low whistle. 'And thank you for trying to get us rescued, my beautiful boy!'

Jazz rose out of the water and tail-walked towards her, waving his flippers as he came near. Then he sank down and swam alongside her, nudging her with his snout.

6

Alfie was the last to plunge into the waves. 'Cool idea,' he said to Pearl, his super-smart friend. She scudded gently towards him, turning to offer him her pearly pink belly to be tickled. 'It wasn't your fault it didn't work. We should have built the lookout fire bigger to start with. That way the sailors might have seen the smoke.'

Pearl twisted in the water and nuzzled him, waiting for him to take hold of her flipper.

'What's up? Are we going for a ride?' he asked. He grabbed her flipper then hitched himself up on to her back. Then he felt her surge ahead. 'Whoo!'

Back near the shore, Fleur grinned broadly and climbed astride Jazz's back. She held on to his dorsal fin. 'Race you,' she yelled to Alfie.

'Wait for me.' Mia clambered on to Stormy then urged him on. 'Come on, what are we waiting for?'

He stared up at her with his small, beady eyes. He didn't join the race – instead he carried Mia to where her hat floated and bobbed. He pushed at it with his nose then dipped his head and came up with the hat perched squarely on his domed head.

'It suits you,' she laughed.

He tossed his head and the hat flew up in the air. She leaned forward and caught it, jammed it on her head then said, 'Come on, Stormy – let's catch up with the others.'

He gave a single, shrill whistle. Then off he surged, carrying Mia on his back, cutting through the waves at top speed, out across the bay. *Race on!*

The crimson sun melted into the horizon. The sea sparkled like a million diamonds. Tomorrow another ship would come, or the day after tomorrow, or the day after that. Right now, as daylight faded, castaways Fleur, Alfie and Mia Fisher made the most of their brilliant time swimming with dolphins.

*

'Why haven't they sent someone to look for us?' Early next morning, Mia sat by the campfire peeling jackfruit for breakfast.

Her dad, James, cooked fish in a pan that Fleur had salvaged from their boat before it sank. 'Who's "they"?'

'I don't know – Granddad or my teachers back home in England. Won't they wonder where we are?'

'Yes, definitely,' he agreed, turning the sizzling fish in the pan. 'The problem is – no one knows exactly where we are. All our electronics onboard *Merlin* were ruined in the storm. A big wave knocked out the navigation station, the radar and the network system all in one go. That's when our signal failed.'

'And that's how come you're here peeling jackfruit instead of sitting behind a desk in school,' Mia's mum, Katie, explained. 'And why Alfie is in the shelter marking our calendar stick and Fleur is collecting firewood from George's cave.'

Mia put the knife and fruit down then trotted into the shelter. 'What day is it?' she asked Alfie.

'Day 18 – Thursday.' Lately he'd improved the calendar stick by carving a notch to show each passing day instead of relying on charcoal to make a mark. Charcoal washed off if the stick got wet, whereas notches were permanent. And he'd worked out how to make the kids' sleeping platform more comfy by stuffing soft, dry grass into the gaps between the bamboo canes. Now all he had to do was find a way to stop insects from crawling over them during the night. He scratched at five new bites on his arm and two on his leg.

'Can we make a boat instead of a new raft?' Mia changed the subject without warning.

'No.' Still scratching, Alfie put on his hat and T-shirt then emerged into the sunlight. 'Is breakfast ready yet?'

'Give me five minutes,' his dad said.

Mia too came out of the shelter and followed up her bright idea. 'Why not? Why can't we build a boat?'

'Because … a million reasons.' A raft was easy – all you needed were bamboo canes lashed together with vines from the jungle that covered the mountain top, and four empty plastic canisters, one on each corner to keep it afloat. A boat, on the other hand, needed proper planks of wood, a saw, screws and nails, a hammer …

Undaunted, Mia turned and sprinted down to George's cave to find Fleur. 'Can we make a boat?' she asked, making George jump. The bright green gecko scuttled off into a dark corner and stared warily at the new arrival.

'What with?' Taking a break from

collecting firewood, Fleur sat on a ledge in the entrance to the cave. She was wearing her white and blue striped T-shirt and shorts. Her feet were bare and her long, wavy auburn hair was tied back from her freckled face with a piece of blue twine.

'Out of a tree trunk,' Mia explained. 'You make it hollow, like they did in the olden days.'

'Like Native Americans?' Fleur frowned, considered the idea then shook her head. 'No – we'd need an axe to chop the tree down then something like a chisel and a hammer to carve out the inside. We haven't got any of those things.'

'Oh.' Mia's face fell.

'Anyway, even if we made a boat, where would we go?' At thirteen, Fleur saw that it was up to her to use some common sense.

'To another island. There are hundreds around here.'

'Yes, and Alfie tried to sail off on the raft to reach one, remember? He got lost and then a storm came and washed him up on another deserted island where there was nothing to eat and no shelter. Pearl and the other dolphins had to rescue him. We won't be trying that again in a hurry.'

Mia grunted then ran back to camp. 'Can we build a boat?' she asked Katie, hopeful as ever.

'Breakfast is ready.' James set the pan down on a rock and invited them to dig in, watched by three yellow-crested cockatoos perched high in one of the nearby palm trees and by a lone macaque monkey squatting on a rock behind the shelter. Higher up the hillside, four other monkeys sat in a row, still as statues.

'Can we?' Mia pestered.

'No, honey – we can't,' Katie replied between mouthfuls of fish. 'Who's on morning lookout duty?'

'Me.' It was Fleur's turn and she was determined, after yesterday, to build the fire bigger and better than ever.

'I'll come up at midday and take over from you,' her dad promised. 'Don't worry – I'll take it easy,' he told Katie. 'I haven't forgotten I'm still recovering from cracked ribs.' He'd received the injury during the shipwreck when he'd been thrown overboard. For the first two weeks on Dolphin Island he'd hardly been able to move. Now he could get about more easily and was keen to do his share.

'While I'm up there, I'll make a big stash of firewood to keep you going through the afternoon,' Fleur decided as she munched her way through a big slice of sweet, yellow fruit. It tasted of a mixture of pineapple and mango, with maybe a hint of banana thrown in. 'OK, I'm done.' She stood up and pushed stray strands of hair behind her ears. 'I'll be keeping a lookout for another ship. Wish me luck, Mia.'

'Good luck.' Quickly Mia ran and gave her a hug then she turned to Alfie. 'OK; if we can't build a boat today, how about we make a new raft?'

'No thanks.' He frowned to ward off memories of being swept out to sea on the last one – the strong, whirling pull of the currents, rain lashing down, waves rising, rolling and breaking over him … 'So how about we explore the island then make a map instead,' he suggested cheerily.

'Cool!' Mia loved this idea. 'Do I get to give names to the places we find?'

'Sure,' Alfie agreed. 'Don't forget your hat. Let's go.'

He set off towards Turtle Beach with Mia in tow.

Fleur smiled at her mum and dad. 'Today's the day that we get rescued,' she vowed. 'A plane or, better still, a coastguard helicopter will fly overhead. Our fire will be bigger and better and they'll spot it. Before you know it, we'll be airlifted out of here, back into civilization.'

'Hot baths,' James said with a sigh. 'A pint of cold beer, a proper bed to sleep in.'

'Clean clothes, shampoo, moisturizer.' Smiling, Katie shared her wish list. 'There's no harm in dreaming,' she added.

'See ya,' Fleur grinned. She set off up the cliff path, stopping to look at a big blue butterfly on a bright red flower then at a black centipede with dark brown spots – the kind that gave you a painful bite. She stepped carefully over it then walked on, looking up at the rocky hillside and the lookout ledge beyond. The sun was already hot in a cloudless sky. Thursday, Day 18 – a perfect day to be rescued.

Chapter Two

The problem with keeping two fires going – one on the beach where the Fishers had built their shelter and one at the lookout point high on the mountain – was the amount of wood it took.

To Fleur it felt like she spent all day every day gathering fuel and stacking it in a dry place. In fact, the whole family constantly picked up driftwood from the beach or dragged fallen branches from the mountain-top jungle.

'This is hard work,' she grumbled to herself as she climbed the hillside under the fierce sun. She'd spent the whole morning stoking the flames and staring out to sea, hoping, hoping … Then, just before the sun reached its midday height, she'd decided to scout further up the mountain for her dad's afternoon supply of fuel. She battled on up the slope, sweating and stumbling across the steep, stony ground then stopped at the edge of the jungle.

'Hi, monkeys,' she said to the band of macaques staring down at her from the branches of the nearest trees. Two of the dark brown creatures swung from their branch and caught hold of hanging vines, swinging themselves along with acrobatic ease. They flicked their long tails and twitched their bushy, grey moustaches, chattering angrily at her before disappearing into deep shadow. 'It's OK, I won't disturb you – I'm only looking for firewood,' she explained.

A mother monkey made sure that her baby didn't stray too far by tucking him under her grey belly and one of the adult males bared his teeth as Fleur advanced.

The jungle was not her favourite place, she had to admit. It was dark and rough underfoot, with creepers and lianas that tripped you up, and there were weird noises made by mysterious animals that she never actually saw – the dark stuff of nightmares that would sometimes wake her with a shock. But there was plenty

17

of firewood lying around so she was determined to carry on.

She entered the shade of the trees and looked up to see two plump pigeons fly noisily from their shady branch out into the sunshine. The male monkey used lianas to swing like Tarzan towards her, almost knocking her off her feet. Fleur ducked, overbalanced and fell against a broad tree trunk. She scraped her shin on a rock then stepped into a stagnant puddle.

'Ouch! Yuck!'

Tarzan Monkey swung towards her a second time, disturbing large fruit bats. Leaves rustled overhead as the bats flitted to safety. 'This is so-o-o yucky,' Fleur decided. 'All I need now is for the monkeys to start chucking things at me.'

It had happened before – nuts were the macaques' favourite weapon. If they did it again and hit their target, Fleur would come out of the jungle with plenty of fresh bruises. 'Please don't,' she said as Tarzan whooshed by and the rest of the gang scampered from branch to branch. 'I know you have to protect your territory, but I'm not the enemy – I promise.'

Mother Monkey tilted her head to one side, as if listening.

'I mean it – I won't hurt you,' Fleur said as she ventured towards a fallen branch lying on the soft ground. 'I actually think you're amazing.'

The mother blinked her white eyelids, relaxed and let go of her baby. She kept careful watch from up high as Fleur lifted the branch.

'Euch!' Fleur jumped back as a giant rat scuttled from its hiding place under the branch. Grey and fat, with black ears and long whiskers, it was almost half a metre long. Once more Fleur lost her balance and this time she stepped into mud that oozed up around her ankles and calves. 'That's it!' she decided. 'I'm out of here.'

So she stumbled from the jungle without the branch, glad to be out of the murky shadows and back in the sunshine in time to see her dad striding towards her.

'I wondered where you'd got to,' he said. 'I was worried about you.'

'I went in there to look for firewood.' Fleur sighed and showed him the graze on her shin. 'Look,' she said.

The shallow wound was dirty and bleeding.

'Does it hurt?' James asked.

'A bit.'

'We need to clean it. Let's go down to the waterfall.'

'What about the fire?' She looked anxiously towards the lookout ledge to see that it was still going strong.

'It'll be OK to leave it for a few minutes.' Her dad insisted on helping her to wash the smarting wound. He led her down to the stream that gurgled from an underwater spring at the top of the cliff path before tumbling over stones to form a small waterfall. 'Sit,' he ordered as he untied the knot in his neckerchief then dipped it in the stream. He dabbed the pale blue cloth on the graze to wipe away mud and grit.

Fleur grimaced and looked away. In the distance she could see Alfie and Mia walking towards base camp after a morning spent exploring Turtle Beach.

'Uh-oh.' James stopped dabbing and examined the leg. 'This is not your lucky day.'

'Why – what's wrong?' She gritted her teeth and made herself look down.

'I can see a little tick attached to your ankle. It's

probably been there a while – he's got his hook in you good and proper.' James examined the tiny insect more closely then placed his thumbnail over it and began to press. 'OK – hold still. If I crush him, I hope that'll sort it.'

'Thanks, Dad.' Fleur sat patiently while he got rid of the tick then dipped the neckerchief into the water again and dabbed the whole area clean. 'I'm sorry I didn't get more firewood like I promised.'

'No problem. There's enough to keep us going until your mum takes over for the night shift. By then I'll have had time to add to the pile. Did you spot any ships?'

'Not one.' Fleur winced again as her dad bandaged the graze with the neckerchief. 'I'm hungry. What's for lunch?'

'Fish for starters, fish for main course and fish for dessert,' he quipped.

'Yum.' Laughing, she stood up, ready to return to camp.

'I'm kidding. You've got coconut for pudding. Watch that leg – take care on your way down.'

'I will,' she promised before saying goodbye and

hurrying back to camp.

'Look what we've got!' Mia exclaimed before Fleur had reached the shelter. She grabbed her hand and dragged her along. 'Alfie and me – we found it lying on Turtle Beach.'

'What is it?' Fleur examined a white fibreglass container with the word *Merlin* printed down one side. There was a wide crack at one end that had let in water.

'It's our lifeboat canister,' Katie explained after she'd persuaded Mia to calm down. In her cut-off jeans and faded pink shirt, barefoot and with her fair hair roughly tied back, she looked as if she'd been a castaway all her life. 'It must have been washed ashore on last night's high tide.'

Fleur stared wide-eyed at Alfie and Mia's new find. Could this be the moment when their hopes of leaving the island and returning to civilization finally became reality? Might they be able to sail to safety after all? At the press of a red button, the canister should open and the lifeboat would automatically inflate. 'Will it still work?'

'I don't know. It's badly cracked, so there may well

be damage on the inside.' Katie set the canister flat in the sand then got ready to press the red button.

'How does it work?' Alfie wanted to know. He leaned over to take a close look, wondering about electronics and computer chips and remembering that his mum knew everything there was to know about boats.

'There's a small, pressurized aerosol in there containing CO_2. It inflates the lifeboat using an automatic pump. The casing breaks apart once the pump springs into action.'

'Cool.' Alfie crossed his fingers then stepped back.

'Shall we try?' Katie asked. 'Ready. Stand clear, everyone.'

She pressed the button. They waited. There was a quiet buzzing noise then nothing. She pressed again. Still nothing, not even a buzz. Gingerly Katie picked up the cracked canister and shook it. It rattled and leaked water out of the crack. 'That's why,' she said softly.

'Huh.' Alfie was the most disappointed. It was the second time their hopes had been dashed in two days and he felt like kicking the stupid thing.

'Never mind,' Fleur muttered. 'Shall we try opening

it up and seeing if we can use what's inside?'

They all agreed and soon the contents of the canister were laid out on the beach – metres of tough, lightweight, waterproof fabric that would have inflated to form the hull, together with a white, three-cornered sail and a bright orange cover that would have made a tent over the top of the boat. There were also two flares for emergencies and a red box full of first-aid supplies such as bandages and sticking plasters.

'Wow, this is really cool.' Alfie cheered up in an instant. He thought of the ways they could use these things – though a closer inspection showed that the fabric of the lifeboat's hull was torn in places, it would still make a great new roof for their leaky shelter. The orange tent could be hung upside down to collect water, or used as a big net to scoop fish out of shallow water.

'Flares.' Fleur picked them up and brushed sand from them. 'We'll have these ready next time we see a ship or a plane.'

Mia grabbed the sail, put it around her shoulders like a cape then paraded along the shoreline.

'So, let's not be too down-hearted,' Katie told them,

picking up the first-aid box and walking back up the beach. 'All this stuff will come in really useful. Good job, Mia and Alfie. Come with me, Fleur. I'll take a look in here and find a clean dressing for that graze on your leg.'

*

That evening, as the sun began to sink, Alfie took Mia and Fleur to a flat rock under the palm trees that surrounded their shelter.

'What are you three up to?' their dad asked. He was busy gutting fish and hanging fillets from a length of wire that he'd suspended above the fire – an experiment to find out if they could smoke their food to make it keep longer.

Katie meanwhile had climbed to the lookout to begin the night watch.

'We're making a map,' Alfie replied. He laid a piece of sail from the boat flat on the smooth rock and held up a long piece of charcoal that he'd pulled from the fire. 'This is the same shape as the island,' he explained. 'Wide at the top and narrow at the bottom.'

'As far as we know.' Fleur reminded him how hard it

was to be sure. Yes, if you went high on to the mountain, you could see that Dolphin Island was roughly a mile and a half long and not more than half a mile wide at any point. And it did taper away at its southern point into a chain of small atolls, stretching out into the ocean.

Alfie used the end of his charcoal stick to draw a rough outline of the island. Then he drew a big black dot on the east coast. 'This is base camp.'

'OK – so there's Turtle Beach.' Fleur pointed to a spot to the south and watched him spell out the words.

'And we know there's a mangrove swamp right down on the southern tip.' Alfie made a third dot on the map, wrote again then sat back with a smile. 'Base Camp Bay, Turtle Beach and Mangrove Bay.'

'Monkey Mountain.' Mia had brought Monkey, her scruffy soft toy, with her and made him comfortable in a niche in the rock. Now she'd decided on the name for the dark, conical peak that towered over everything. 'And this is Misty Island.' She pointed to the largest of the atolls to the south.

'And Lookout Point.' Alfie made a mark a little way

inland from Base Camp Bay.

'What about George's Cave?' Mia asked.

Alfie nodded then marked a spot on the eastern end of the same bay.

'Speaking of which – look who's here.' Glancing up, Fleur grinned as she spotted George creeping along the rock to sit next to Monkey. He perched with his head raised and his toes splayed, watching their every move. 'M-A-P, map,' she explained carefully.

'Yeah – like, he understands!' Alfie grinned. 'From now on, every time we find a new place, we'll make up a name for it,' he decided.

'Waterfall!' Mia remembered one that they'd missed.

'Yes, that can be Butterfly Falls.' Fleur decided it was her turn to make up names. 'And what about Echo Cave Beach for the cove to the north of us?' This was where Alfie had discovered some big plastic containers amongst the seaweed and driftwood. It had a dark cave under the cliff that you could walk into, and if you shouted it made a spooky echo.

'Cool.' Alfie wrote carefully then laid down the charcoal. Making the map made him feel safer somehow. Now anyone could say, 'I'm off to Echo Cave,' or 'I'm going fishing on Turtle Beach,' and everyone else would know exactly where they were. 'Where shall we put it? Somewhere nice and dry.'

'Come on – let's hang it on the wall, next to Dad's hammock,' Fleur suggested, limping a little as she led the way.

It was agreed. The new map of Dolphin Island would have pride of place inside the shelter.

'Excellent,' James said when Mia showed him the map before they hung it up. 'And what's the plan for tomorrow?'

'New roof,' Alfie told him. 'We'll make one out of the material from the lifeboat.'

'And we'll go fishing with our new orange net.' Fleur looked forward to a good haul.

'Catch as many as you like.' James explained that smoking the fish seemed to be working. 'We can hang them up inside the shelter for safe-keeping once they're cooked all the way through – to keep them away from marauding monkeys.'

'Tomorrow I want to go swimming with Stormy,'

Mia said hopefully then yawned.

'If they show up.' Fleur added a note of caution.

'Oh yes – let's not forget the dolphins,' James said with a smile. 'You're tired, Mia. It's bedtime.'

'Uh-oh, Monkey!' Mia remembered that she'd left her soft toy on the rock.

'You lie down. I'll fetch him,' Fleur said quickly. She stepped out of the shelter in time to catch the very last rays of the sun. One bright star had already appeared in the darkening sky. She paused to take in the sound of waves lapping the shore and the sight of the lookout fire glowing on the hillside.

In her head, she ran through the plans for tomorrow – new roof, fishing, swimming. Day 19. The lone star glittered as she walked to the rock to fetch Monkey. Her head swam a little and she felt thirsty. 'Hey, George,' she murmured to her friendly gecko. 'Sorry, I don't have any food for you.'

George tilted his flat head and whisked his lizard tail from side to side.

'Tomorrow,' Fleur promised. 'I'll bring you smoked fish – yummy!'

Chapter Three

Alfie woke up next morning thinking about food. Salt and vinegar crisps, burgers, sausage rolls – everything tasty that was bad for you. He lay on his back inside the shelter, staring up at the roof made from woven palm fronds, his mouth watering. Chocolate creme eggs, pizza, spaghetti bolognese.

'Are you awake?' Fleur whispered. She'd woken up before dawn and lay quietly so as not to disturb the others. Now she heard Alfie stir.

'Sausage rolls,' he said out loud.

'Huh? What are you on about?'

'Food – if we had a magic wand that could make anything in the world appear on Dolphin Island, what would you choose?'

Fleur thought for ages. 'A chocolate brownie,' she

said at last with a sigh of longing. 'Topped with squirty whipped cream.'

'A bag of Haribos.' A still-sleepy Mia joined the daydream. 'The sugary ones that taste like Coca-Cola – I'd save those until last.'

'Cool.' Alfie stretched then rolled off his mattress on to the floor. He crawled out of the shelter on to the sand, then stood up and fed the fire with a couple of pieces of driftwood, glancing up at Lookout Point to see that the fire up there was still burning steadily. His mum saw him and waved.

He waved back, stretched again and wandered off down the beach, picking up small shells and keeping the ones he liked. In amongst the bright yellow seaweed at the water's edge, he found a shiny red bottle top and a handy length of blue twine which he pocketed. His next find was an orange plastic juice bottle, complete with cap. He quickly transferred the shells into the bottle and pressed the cap back on, enjoying the feel of the cool sea breeze on his face and water lapping around his ankles.

Soon Fleur and Mia joined him, wearing swimsuits,

ready for an early morning swim.

'Last one into the water has to collect coconuts!' Mia challenged as she threw herself in.

Collecting coconuts from under the palm trees was a boring job – much less fun than scaling the cliff to collect gulls' eggs, crabbing in the rock pools or climbing up to Butterfly Falls to collect fresh water. So Fleur and Alfie plunged together into the waves. They ran until they were waist-deep then started to swim – Alfie in an untidy front crawl as he clutched the bottle containing the shells. Fleur swam in a neat breaststroke until they caught up with Mia.

'It was a draw.' Fleur turned on to her back and sculled gently to stay afloat. High in the cloudless sky she saw a silver dot leaving a thin trail of white in its wake. 'Plane,' she noted casually. Not that she intended to do anything about it.

'Where?' Mia demanded eagerly.

'Due south, right over Misty Island.' Alfie swam alongside her. He too had spotted the aircraft. 'Don't get your hopes up, Mi-mi – it's flying too high for anyone to see us.'

'Are you sure?' To Mia, any plane flying over the island was a reason to get excited. 'Can't we set off one of those flare thingies we found yesterday?'

Alfie set her straight with a few facts. 'Mia, that plane is probably a Boeing 747 or an Airbus 380 cruising at 36,000 feet. From up there, the whole of Dolphin Island looks like a tiny speck amongst hundreds of other tiny specks. They won't even see the smoke from our fires, let alone a little flare.'

Mia was upset but soon cheered up by the sight of three dolphins rounding the Turtle Beach headland. Pearl, Stormy and Jazz were here for early morning fun and games.

'Hurray!' Mia yelled as she trod water and slapped the surface with both palms. The splash attracted Stormy's attention and he circled her, full of curiosity about what she would do next. Meanwhile, Jazz swam to say hi to Fleur and Pearl performed a few spectacular lob-tail splashes for Alfie's benefit.

'Hey, you're drowning me!' he yelled as white spray rained down.

Pearl took no notice. She whacked her tail flukes

against the water again, churning up the surface and swimming in circles around poor Alfie until at last she relented and came towards him for a stroke of her pearly pink belly.

Laughing, he rattled the orange bottle in her face. 'What's this?' he cried. 'What's making this noise?'

Pearl clapped her jaws together then nudged the bottle with her snout. Alfie whisked it away then tapped the top of her head with it. She rolled over on to her back, waving her flippers and giving her birdlike, chirping call for Stormy and Jazz to join them. Alfie rubbed her belly then tossed the bottle into the air. Would it float when it came down? he wondered. Or would it sink?

The shells inside the bottle rattled then the bottle landed. It bobbed on the surface until Stormy rushed forward and flipped it sideways with his nose. Then Jazz took the bottle in his jaws and leaped clear of the water, carrying it away. With Alfie, Fleur and Mia looking on, Pearl and Stormy gave chase, soon catching up with Jazz, who flipped the bottle straight up into the air. Pearl made a clean catch between her teeth then returned triumphant to Alfie.

'Cool!' he cried, grabbing the bottle from her and rattling it again. It was like throwing a stick for a dog, only a million times more fun. 'That's one point to Pearl and me.' He threw the bottle as high as he could and they all laughed when Stormy, the quickest of the three, nipped in front of Jazz and Pearl to catch it and swim away with it before flipping it up on to the end of his snout and balancing it there.

'Quick, Stormy – bring it here,' Mia called as she slapped the surface with her palms.

Her dolphin swam with the bottle and dropped it in front of her.

'Pearl and Alfie, one – Mia and Stormy, one.' Fleur launched herself towards Mia and grabbed the bottle. 'OK, Jazz – I'm relying on you!' She threw the bottle further than ever and watched him leap clear of the water ahead of the other two. He seized it and swam back, swift as an arrow. 'Jazz and me, one!' she cried in delight.

And so they played their new game of fetch – three kids and three dolphins in the turquoise ocean, above a reef of pink coral, under a cloudless sky.

'We won!' Mia returned to camp triumphant. 'Three to me and Stormy, two to Pearl and Alfie and two to Fleur and Jazz. That means I'm the winner.'

'Here – eat this.' Katie had swapped places with James, who was now on lookout duty high on the hill. She handed Mia a piece of smoked fish and a chunk of white coconut flesh.

Alfie took off his wet T-shirt and laid it flat on a rock to dry. His skinny body looked tanned against the faded red of his swimming shorts and his brown hair was bleached by the sun. 'You should have seen the dolphins go after the bottle,' he told his mum. 'They shot through the water at I don't know how many nautical miles per hour.'

'I'm glad you all had a nice time.' As she handed out the breakfast, Katie noticed that the dressing on Fleur's graze had washed off in the sea so she went to the first-aid box to fetch a new one. 'This is looking a bit nasty,' she commented as she examined Fleur's leg. The wound was red and the area of skin around it was puffy. 'How's it feel?'

'Still sore,' Fleur admitted. 'It stung when I went into the water.'

So Katie dabbed it with antiseptic cream from the box and carefully covered it with another plaster, bigger than the first. And after breakfast, when it came to sharing out the day's jobs, she insisted on giving Fleur the easy, boring one of collecting coconuts while Mia fetched gulls' eggs and water and Alfie went fishing with the new orange lifeboat cover. He came back at noon with a good catch of two medium-sized groupers and an eel measuring almost half a metre.

'That'll keep us going for a while, but I think we'll have eggs for lunch,' Katie decided. 'Scrambling eggs is quicker and easier than cooking fish. Then, when the sun goes down a bit, we can get on with making our new roof.'

Fleur was as keen as the others to fix the roof, but when the time came she found she had hardly enough energy to climb on to the rock behind the shelter and wait there to catch the wide strips of fabric cut from the damaged lifeboat.

What's wrong with me? she wondered as Alfie flung

the pale grey fabric over the top of the palm frond roof and she reached out to catch it.

'Pull,' he told her. 'I've kept hold of this end. That's it – pull harder.'

Fleur knew that it was an important job. The aim was to make the roof stronger and more watertight so she had to find a way of fastening down her end of the fabric so it didn't blow away in a storm. This was tricky – the only way she could do it was to use a sharp knife to pierce holes in the cloth then strip leaves from a creeper and thread it through the holes. Then she lashed the whole thing on to the existing roof structure. Alfie did the same at his end.

'I'm bored,' Mia announced after they'd been working on the roof for a while. She'd spent the time threading shells on to a thin piece of string for a necklace to add to the three she'd already made.

Katie was standing by with the next wide strip of fabric which would overlap the one before. 'Why not take Monkey to see Daddy?'

'Where is he?'

'Up on Lookout Point. Tell him the work on the roof

39

is coming along fine.'

So Mia took Monkey up the cliff path past Butterfly Falls and spent the rest of the afternoon on the ledge with James, telling him about the game they'd played with the dolphins while he kept the fire going and they both watched out for ships and planes.

'It's Friday,' he reminded her as they gazed out to sea. Below them they could hear the waterfall tumbling over rocks and below that was the canopy of palm trees hiding their shelter from view. 'Almost three weeks since we got here.'

'It's been ages and ages,' Mia said with a sigh.

James looked closely at Mia – at the bright feathers in her hat and at her small, delicate features half hidden by the brim. Sometimes he overlooked how young she was and that it was his job to keep up her spirits. 'Yes, and I bet you're forgetting everything you've learned at school – reading and writing, numbers,' he said with a twinkle in his eye.

'No!' she retorted. 'You can test me if you like. Go on, test me.'

'OK, what's fifteen add nine?'

'Twenty-four.' It took her a while but she got there with the help of fingers and toes.

'Good. Why not take off one of your necklaces and use shells to count with? What's twenty-four add five?'

The shells helped. 'Twenty-nine,' Mia answered confidently.

'Correct. Thirteen take away seven?'

'Six.'

Thousands of miles away from her classroom in grey old England, Mia's Friday afternoon maths lesson went on to the sound of gulls screeching and the sight of pelicans landing on the headland, of monkeys scampering across the hillside and cockatoos calling raucously from the palm trees below.

*

'You know Mangrove Bay?' Alfie mentioned to Fleur after they'd finished the roof at last and Katie had gone up to Lookout Point to do the usual evening swap with James. The sun was sinking and a cool breeze came in from the east – a relief after the sweltering heat of the afternoon.

'Yes, 'course.' Fleur just wanted to sit and relax by

the campfire – not talk. She felt hot and a little bit dizzy.

'OK, so tomorrow I reckon we should pack food and water and trek down there.'

'Who should?' she asked wearily.

'You and me. It's too far for Mia.'

'What for?' She wouldn't admit it, but right now, the idea of trailing down to the southern tip of Dolphin Island with the sun beating down on them made her feel faint.

'For a start, we'd be able to make a better map,' he explained. 'We'd be like European explorers in the sixteenth century, landing on the east coast of America, finding out where the bays and headlands are.'

'Yeah, that'd be cool,' she admitted.

'Plus, we might find more fruit in places we haven't visited yet – who knows, maybe melons and grapes even.'

'Really?' Fleur's voice rose in disbelief. 'This island is deserted, remember. Nobody lives here. So who would've planted stuff like that?'

Alfie stuck to his guns. 'Seeds can be washed ashore or get blown by the wind. Sometimes birds poo them out. They grow without anybody planting them, silly.'

'Really,' Fleur said again, this time in a low, flat voice intended to show she wasn't interested. Honestly, she just wanted to lie down and go to sleep.

'OK, so maybe sugarcane.' He went on in a more realistic way. 'That would be good, wouldn't it? We could cut it down and carry it back. And if we did happen to find grape vines growing in one of the inlets, we could dry the grapes to make raisins then store them as long as we liked.'

'Dream on,' Fleur said with a sigh. All Alfie ever thought about these days was his stomach. 'Listen – do you mind if we talk about this tomorrow? And when Dad gets back with Mia, can you tell him I went to bed early? Ask Mia not to wake me up.'

'Will do. Are you OK?' he asked as she stood up and slowly made her way inside the shelter.

'Yep – just tired.' And hot but shivering at the same time, which was weird. Fleur sank down on to her sleeping platform and straight away closed her eyes.

Alfie followed her in. 'Sure?'

'Sure,' she insisted. 'I'll get a good night's sleep then

I'll be fine. We'll talk about that trek to Mangrove Bay tomorrow – OK?'

'Cool. Goodnight then.' He left the shelter and strolled down the beach to see if he could spot dolphins before night fell.

'G'night,' Fleur murmured. Her head ached and her throat felt sore, but the sound of the waves soon lulled her to sleep and by the time Mia and her dad arrived in camp, Fleur was dead to the world.

Chapter Four

'What's wrong with Fleur?' Mia asked Alfie as they climbed over the headland early next morning to Echo Cave Beach. Fleur had set off with them but had only made it as far as George's Cave before she'd stopped to rest. 'Is she poorly?'

'A bit, I reckon.' He led the way over the rocks on to the beach where he'd found the big canisters that they'd used to keep their raft afloat – the one that had drifted out to sea. The beach was about two hundred metres wide, littered along the high-tide line with mounds of seaweed and debris from passing ships – a treasure-trove of old ropes, cans, car tyres, flip-flops and plastic. At the edge of the beach there was an overhanging rock leading to the deep cave – a safe place to shelter from the many strong winds and storms that swept in from the sea and hit the tropical island, often without warning. 'Hurry up, Mia. We promised Dad we wouldn't be long.'

The first job this morning, before he and Fleur set out on their trek to the south of the island, was to scout the whole width of Echo Cave Beach for more driftwood for the fires. The wood was easy to spot from a distance – old planks and logs that had floated in on the tide, broken doors and pieces of timber from buildings destroyed by tsunamis and earthquakes – they all stood out amongst the jumbled heaps of seaweed and shells.

Mia caught up with Alfie then ran ahead into Echo Cave. 'Coo-ee!' she called.

'Coooo-eeee!' A faint echo came back.

Mia laughed then reappeared on the beach dragging a long piece of timber covered in flaking white paint. 'How about this?'

'Cool.' He pointed to a rotten plank and a heavy branch that he'd dragged from the heaps of seaweed. 'Stack it there with the other things. The sooner we collect enough wood and carry it back to base camp, the sooner me and Fleur can set off. If she's not too sick, that is.'

'She didn't have any breakfast,' Mia reminded him. 'She only drank some water.'

'I know. That's not like her.'

'She didn't even want to talk to George.'

'Yeah, that's right.' The hopeful gecko had arrived at camp soon after dawn. He'd waited patiently for Fleur to pet him and feed him scraps of fruit, but she'd ignored him and wandered into the shelter while the rest of the family ate.

Then the greedy macaques had arrived, swinging down from the palm trees and snatching the pieces of jackfruit that James had peeled and sliced. James had stood up, waved his arms and yelled at them. One of the departing monkeys had decided to bare her teeth at George, who'd shot off down the beach and taken refuge in his cave.

'It wasn't like Fleur not to stick up for poor George either,' Alfie realized. 'Come on – we've got enough for now. Let's go back.'

So they dragged their wood along the beach, leaving

grooves in the smooth sand. Then they hoisted it on to their shoulders and climbed over the headland, to find Fleur sitting at the entrance to George's Cave, exactly where they'd left her. George was there, sunning himself on a nearby rock.

'Hey.' Alfie lowered his load on to the sand next to Fleur. 'How are you feeling?'

'Good,' she murmured.

'You don't look it.' Her face was pale and there were dark circles under her eyes.

'I'm a bit thirsty, that's all.' Actually, the night's sleep hadn't helped one bit. It still felt as if there were little men with hammers inside her head, knocking away at her skull. And she couldn't get rid of the hot, twitchy feeling she'd noticed as she fell asleep.

'So what about our expedition?' Alfie guessed what Fleur's answer would be.

'Not today,' she mumbled. 'Maybe tomorrow.'

'I'll come.' Mia was quick to volunteer. 'Please – I won't be a nuisance.'

'Let her,' Fleur said. She fancied a day to herself,

without having to keep an eye on their little sister.

Alfie nodded and reluctantly agreed. 'OK, then.'

'Yay!' Mia jumped up and down. She raced up the beach to tell her mum. 'I'm going with Alfie to Mangrove Bay.'

Katie made sure that both Mia and Alfie were wearing plenty of sunblock from the bottle that had washed ashore after *Merlin* sank. She checked that they were carrying bottles of water in their rucksack. 'Stay safe,' she insisted. 'Stick to the shore and don't try swimming around any headlands. Remember there are dangerous currents out there.'

'How could I forget?' Alfie said with a shudder. He'd found out the hard way when he'd set sail on the raft.

'Have you got a sharp knife?'

'Two – one for me and one for Mia.' Knives always came in handy – to slash your way through thickets of bamboo or mangrove swamps, for instance.

'Don't lose it, Mi-mi.' Katie gave Mia a quick hug then sent her on her way. 'Stay with Alfie and don't do anything silly.'

'Bye!' Mia beamed back at her.

'Thanks for fetching the firewood,' Katie told Alfie. She was proud of how well he was doing now that he'd got over his fear of water – all thanks to Pearl. He seemed to have grown two inches and to walk with his head up and shoulders back, ready to tackle any challenge that the island threw at him.

'That's OK – bye.' He set off quickly, the rucksack slung over one shoulder, striding out towards Turtle Beach.

'What's Fleur up to, by the way?' Katie flung a question at him as he departed.

'She's chilling then maybe going for a swim,' Alfie reported over his shoulder, pushing to the back of his mind any worries he might have about his big sister.

Katie glanced down the beach and saw Fleur lounging by George's Cave. *Hmm, that's not like her*, she said to herself, echoing Alfie's earlier thought as she set off up the cliff to fetch water. *Still, I can't blame her. Fleur works hard, day in, day out, doing all her chores and looking after Mia. She definitely deserves some downtime.*

*

'Bye, Fleur!' Mia yelled from the headland leading to Turtle Beach.

By this time Fleur had left George's Cave and stood ankle-deep in the water. She waved Mia goodbye. The waves lapped against the shore. The sun rose higher. Nothing disturbed the sandpipers feeding in the rock pools or the gannets dropping like stones from the sky and plunging head-first into the water, coming up with fish between their beaks. Perfect peace and quiet – this was what Fleur needed today.

Meanwhile, though she was small and slight, Mia found it easy to keep up with Alfie, who kept stopping to look at interesting shells and the broad tracks made by turtles in their slow crawl out of the water on to the sand where they would lay their eggs. He measured out the width of Turtle Beach with long strides – roughly one metre per stride and he counted to one hundred and fifty, which meant that Turtle Beach was that many metres wide. 'Remember that number so we can put it on the map,' he told Mia as they rounded the next headland and he began counting again.

Mia was more interested in paddling and in jumping

51

over shallow waves as they broke on the shore until suddenly Alfie stopped mid-stride and pointed towards some cliffs overlooking the new beach. 'Over there – a cave.'

Mia looked and saw a dark entrance between two rock pinnacles. Caves were interesting – they usually had useful things in them and were good places to hide. So she and Alfie left off the important job of measuring the bay and scooted up the beach to investigate.

'I reckon it's even deeper than Echo Cave,' Alfie said as they came to the entrance. He stooped to look beyond a fallen boulder wedged between the two tall rocks that blocked part of the entrance. The inside of the cave was dry, with loose pebbles scattered across a level floor.

'Let's go in.' Without waiting for Alfie to give the go-ahead, Mia crawled in, grunting as she squeezed under the boulder into a big chamber. 'Cooee!' she called and waited for an echo. No sound came back. 'It's really quiet in here. And I can't see,' she complained.

Alfie slithered in on his belly then stood up and

took a deep breath. 'I don't think the waves reach this far – it doesn't smell of seaweed or anything. It's a cool cave, though, if we ever need to shelter from a storm.'

'Or play hide and seek. Can we give it a name?'

'Like what?' For a while, nothing came to mind in the calm, silent blackness. Then he had an idea. 'How about Mystery Cave – 'cos we've never seen it before and we can't work out how big it is or how far back it goes. It could go on for hundreds of metres underground for all we know.'

Mia was thrilled. Her eyes widened and she clapped her hands. 'Alfie, what if there's a big treasure-chest hidden in here with jewels inside?'

'Brought ashore by pirates in the olden days. Why not?' For once he was happy to let his imagination run wild. 'Pirates with big cutlasses and pistols. A treasure-chest with stolen diamonds and rubies and doubloons.'

'What are dub-looms?'

'Doubloons. They're ancient gold coins. Pirates stole them then stashed them away in caves where no one could find them.'

'Whoo!' Mia did a little dance and chanted, 'Pirate

Cave, Pirate Cave, full of treasure!'

Alfie laughed. 'OK, you win – Pirate Cave it is. Come on, let's go. We've still got lots of exploring to do.'

Crawling out into the sunshine, they had to wait for their eyes to get used to the bright light. Then Alfie took a bottle of water from his rucksack and they both took a long swig before setting off again in the direction of Mangrove Bay.

The sun was high now and, as they covered fresh ground, they tried to keep to the shade of the cliffs and palm trees that fringed the bays.

'Just think – we could be the very first people who ever walked on this beach.' Alfie stopped and pointed back at their trail of footprints in the smooth sand. A light wind rustled through the palm trees growing close to the water's edge and two tree kangaroos clung to one of the trunks, their long, thick tails dangling. 'How cool is that!'

'Very cool.' Mia grinned up at him from under the brim of her hat.

They trekked on, feeling on top of the world, until they came to a cove only about twenty metres across and bordered by steep rocks that they had to scale before they could look down on to a patch of dazzling white sand where nothing grew and the only signs of life were dozens of big black crabs scuttling between pools in the dark red rocks.

Alfie didn't like the look of the descent on to the beach, still less the sheer cliff they would have to climb at the far side of the cove. The only other way would be to wade into the sea then swim around the two rocky headlands to find out what lay beyond. But their mum had given strict instructions. *Beware dangerous currents and riptides. No swimming.*

He frowned. The day so far had been a big adventure but it looked as if their expedition had come to a full stop. 'That's it,' he told Mia in a voice that showed there was no point arguing. 'Black Crab Cove is as far as we get.'

*

Back at Base Camp Bay, Fleur took a nap in George's Cave. She woke up feeling hot and sticky and was soon tempted out into the cool, clear water. She crossed the hot sand under a scorching sun, waded in then swam slowly out into the bay. *If only my head would stop throbbing*, she thought. But it felt good to let the salt water buoy her up so that all she needed to do was kick gently with her legs to stay afloat. She swam for a while then rolled on to her back and floated with her arms outspread, looking up at the blue sky without a thought in her head. She didn't notice Jazz until he swam close enough to nudge her with his snout.

'Hey.' She turned her head and smiled at him.

Jazz gave a low whistle and nuzzled close. He had a funny, down-turned mouth that gave him a serious expression, and the dark shading round his eyes made it look as if he was wearing sunglasses. Today her sweet-natured dolphin did none of his acrobatic leaps, preferring to swim quietly beside Fleur until she decided that it was time to play.

'Where are the others?' she murmured as she glanced out to sea. She saw Pearl with her mother, Marina, circling the reef where *Merlin* had come to grief, and further out she caught a glimpse of Stormy and the rest of the pod. 'We had a great game yesterday, didn't we?'

Jazz clicked and creaked his reply. He nudged her again then offered her his flipper.

'Sorry – no games today,' she sighed. 'I'm not feeling very well.'

It was as if Jazz knew what she was saying. He cuddled up to her and allowed her to slide an arm across his back then he steered her slowly towards the beach.

'Thanks,' Fleur muttered weakly. As a matter of fact, she'd started to feel really dizzy. She blinked and when she opened her eyes, everything looked blurred – the shoreline and the beach, George's Cave, the palm trees and the shelter. 'Oh,' she groaned. She let her arm slip from Jazz's back and felt herself start to sink.

Jazz acted quickly. He dived under her, took her weight then raised her to the surface, keeping her slumped across his back as he swam on. Behind him, Stormy and Pearl gathered. They whacked the water with their tail flukes and whistled loudly.

Up at the shelter, Katie heard the dolphins' call and glanced up. She was busy smashing open a coconut shell and prising out the flesh, ready for Mia and Alfie when they decided they'd had enough of exploring the island. The first thing she saw was the spray made by Pearl and Stormy and after that Jazz carrying Fleur towards the shore.

In an instant Katie realized what was happening. She dropped the coconut and sprinted down the beach.

Close to the shore, Fleur groaned and slipped underwater a second time. Her limbs wouldn't work and the sun was a ball of fire burning her eyes. The whole world had tilted and she sank below the waves until once more Jazz came to her rescue, lifting her up until her face cleared the water and she was able to gasp and drag air into her lungs.

Katie ran into the waves, swam out then took a firm hold of Fleur. With Jazz, Pearl and Stormy looking on, she swam with her back to the shore.

Fleur's eyes were closed; her arms and legs hung limp.

'Wake up,' Katie urged. Clear of the water, she struggled to lift and carry Fleur, only getting as far as George's Cave before she had to set her down against a rock. She put her fingers against Fleur's wrist and felt her pulse then leaned in and listened to her breathing. 'OK, honey – open your eyes,' she pleaded as she stroked strands of wet hair from her cheek.

Fleur's eyelids fluttered open. She saw the blurred outline of her mum's features close to her own and heard the high call of the dolphins waiting anxiously at the water's edge.

'You went for a swim and you fainted,' Katie murmured. 'But you're better now.'

Fleur nodded. When she tried to stand, her legs wobbled and wouldn't take her weight so she fell back against the rock.

'It's all right – no rush. Take your time.' Gently Katie pushed Fleur's head forward until it rested between her knees, hoping this would help her feel less dizzy. 'It's a good job Jazz was there. Otherwise I dread to think what would have happened. How do you feel now?'

'Better,' Fleur decided. 'I don't understand – why did I faint?'

'I don't know – maybe it was the heat.' Katie helped her to her feet and supported her as they began to walk slowly up the beach. 'It could be a touch of sunstroke. Or maybe it was something you ate that's disagreed with you.'

In her mind, Katie went through other possibilities – malaria from a mosquito bite, typhoid from polluted water. These were only two of the many nasty tropical diseases that came to mind, but she kept these thoughts to herself as she led Fleur into the shelter. 'I want you to drink lots of water then lie down,' she insisted. 'Rest here while I go up to Lookout Point and tell your dad what's happened.'

Chapter Five

There was no escape from the heat. The midday sun was fierce and even in the shade temperatures could soar to forty degrees centigrade and beyond. Fleur tossed and turned on her mattress to find a comfortable position but when she closed her eyes and tried to sleep, she heard noises inside the shelter that kept her awake – quiet rustling and scraping, louder knocking and crunching, all backed by the ceaseless sound of waves pounding against rocks as the tide came in.

She opened her eyes. The knocking, crunching noise was made by a macaque. He'd ventured into the shelter to steal one of the coconuts stashed by the door, hitting it hard against a stone to smash the shell then munching his way through the flesh inside. Fleur stared at him and he stared back without blinking.

Squatting on his hind legs, he twitched his tail and curled his top lip to expose his teeth.

'Shoo!' Fleur said weakly.

The monkey ignored her and carried on eating.

Uhh! Fleur was too exhausted to sit up and make him scram. She closed her eyes again and drifted off to sleep.

In her dream there were brown monkeys everywhere. They ran riot in gangs of twenty or more – over the shelter's new roof, stamping on it then tearing it apart. They were inside the shelter, swinging from James's hammock and smashing the bamboo mattresses, squealing with rage and breaking everything in sight.

Hordes of macaques – hundreds of them – overran the beach. They scooped crabs out of rock pools and used stones to smash their shells. They danced jigs on the rocky headlands then picked up pebbles and pelted poor George inside his cave. Their squeals deafened her but there was worse to come. Something huge and silent lumbered out of the dark jungle and made its way down the mountain towards the fire on Lookout

Point. It was bigger than a gorilla, walking on its hind legs and swinging its long arms. Its dark eyes glittered in the firelight as it put its hand in the flames and drew out a burning branch, raised it above its massive head then flung it high into the night sky. Sparks fell and faded. The creature opened its mouth and roared.

Fleur gasped and sat up. Daylight flooded into the shelter. Mia stood in the doorway.

'We're back,' she announced as she darted across the shelter to study the map hanging on the wall behind the hammock.

Fleur let out a loud sigh of relief. Her nightmare had left her shaking and sweating with fear and the normal, everyday sight of a smiling Mia in her hat, T-shirt and shorts made Fleur want to jump up and hug her.

'Where's Mum?' Mia demanded.

'Still with Dad on Lookout Point, I guess.'

'We found a new cave here,' Mia reported as she pointed to the map. 'We called it Pirate Cave 'cos there could be treasure inside. And Black Crab Cove – that's down here. On the way home we found two sponges on Turtle Beach.'

Alfie came into the shelter and put down his rucksack. 'How are you doing?' he asked Fleur.

'Not good,' she admitted for the first time, resting back on her elbows. She saved the part about fainting and being rescued by Jazz for later, in case Mia got worried. 'I'd never even have made it past Turtle Beach, the way I feel right now.'

'Have you had anything to eat? Do you want some coconut?'

Fleur grimaced and sank back on to her mattress. Her elbows hurt and every other joint in her body ached too. 'No thanks.'

'Let's show Fleur the sponges.' Non-stop Mia delved into the rucksack and produced two of them, each about ten centimetres wide. 'See – nice and squishy!'

'Cool,' Fleur said softly as she let her eyelids flutter and close.

'Ssshh!' Alfie warned and he led Mia outside. 'Fleur wants to sleep. We'll go and tell Mum and Dad that we're back.'

Fleur heard them walk away. Their voices grew faint, drowned out by the sound of the sea. She drifted off again, into the world of nightmare.

The giant beast lumbered towards her. Its weight caused an avalanche of loose stones down the side of the mountain. She couldn't make out what kind of creature it was. It had claws and a shaggy black coat like a bear but it walked like a man. The ground shook as it came closer and closer. When it roared, the ferocious sound filled her head and its open mouth was a red cave. Saliva dribbled from its yellow fangs.

Fleur woke with a start and a shudder, her mouth dry, her forehead dripping with sweat. There was a flash of bright green on the wall then the map swung off its hook and fell to the floor.

'George!' Fleur groaned.

He shot out from under the map and sprinted for the door.

Was he real or was he part of her dream? She didn't turn her head to see where he went, because what did it matter? All she wanted to do was sleep without dreaming. Sleep, sleep, sleep.

*

Katie and James racked their brains. They sat together

at Lookout Point, trying to figure out what could be wrong with Fleur.

'At first I thought it might be a touch of sunstroke,' Katie said. She poked the fire with a long stick, shielding her face from the heat with her other hand. 'That could explain why she fainted, couldn't it?'

'It might,' James agreed. 'But she was off her food earlier this morning – that was before she'd been out in the sun.'

'So – food poisoning?' Katie tried out her second theory.

'Has she been sick?'

'No, not as far as I know.'

'Diarrhoea?'

'No.'

'So not food poisoning then.' James chewed his lip and came up with another answer. 'That graze on her leg looked pretty nasty. I was there just after she did it. Maybe I didn't remove the tick properly.'

'Yeah, and the dressing came off when she went swimming. It could have got infected then.' This seemed likely to Katie. 'We'll have to smother it with antiseptic cream and keep it dry and covered up from now on – even if that's shutting the stable door after the horse has bolted.'

James agreed. 'I'll go down and take another look at it,' he decided, standing up just as Mia and Alfie appeared by the waterfall. 'Don't worry too much,' he told Katie.

'I'll try not to. It's just that this makes me realize how cut off we are. There's no chance of getting Fleur to a doctor if she gets worse.' For the first time since they'd arrived on Dolphin Island, Katie felt helpless. 'We don't have the right medicines to treat malaria, for example – if that's what it turns out to be.'

James waved at Mia, who charged ahead of Alfie. 'It's not malaria,' he said a touch too sharply because the very word scared him. 'We were all taking our anti-malarial tablets until we were shipwrecked, remember?'

'You're right.' Katie put on a cheerful face as Mia drew near. 'Go and have a chat with Fleur and give her a cuddle. I'll keep these two occupied.'

*

It was no good – no way could Fleur get back to sleep.

She would drift off towards slumber then suddenly drop off a ledge down a deep, dark hole – a sensation that made her gasp and open her eyes, clutching the mattress and trying to catch her breath.

She sat up and stared out of the shelter at a bank of white clouds gathering on the horizon. Perhaps it would rain. The clouds might darken and build up to a storm. That's what normally happened – the sky would turn dark; a wind would blow in from the sea. It would grow stronger, tear palm fronds from the trees and whip the beautiful white paradise beach into a whirling, blinding sandstorm.

As she stared at the clouds, the outline of her dad appeared in the doorway. He stooped to come in then sat cross-legged beside her. 'I hear you fainted and gave your mum a fright,' he said.

'Yeah – sorry.'

'No need to say sorry. It wasn't your fault.'

'Good job Jazz was there,' they both said at once then smiled.

'We think the graze on your leg might be what's causing the problem,' he went on. 'Do you mind if I take another look?'

'OK.' Fleur closed her eyes and wrinkled her nose as he peeled back the plaster.

James tutted at what he saw then quickly covered the wound again. 'Are you still feeling dizzy?'

'Yeah and I've got achy joints.'

'Bad headache?'

'The worst. And my arms and legs itch.'

'Any rash?' He ran his hand lightly along her arm then looked closely. 'Yep, that's definitely a rash.'

'What do you think it is, Dad?'

'I'm not sure,' he admitted. 'I'm no doctor, but I've just made a connection. You remember that tick I found on your ankle?'

'Yes. Disgusting,' she said with a shiver.

'You probably picked him up on one of your firewood forays into the jungle. That's where ticks like him hang out, in bushes and leaf litter.'

'Yuck!' she said, shivering again.

'Well, I tried to get rid of him for you, but maybe I didn't do a very good job. Besides which, the bite was close to the graze on your shin. Let me take a closer look.'

Fleur gritted her teeth for a second examination.

'Just as I thought.' James leaned back and patted her hand. 'There's a tiny black mark where the tick bit you – a little ulcer. Normally the bite carries an infection but your body deals with it so that you hardly know it's happened – you're just left with the black spot, like a spider bite. But it's your bad luck that you grazed your leg and opened up a wound for the infection to travel further into your system and make everything more serious.'

'How serious?'

'I won't lie, Fleury – it's not a nice illness. It's a type of blood poisoning. This rash will get worse and you'll start to feel feverish.'

'I already do,' she groaned, holding on to his hand and trying not to cry.

'What you've got is called tick-bite fever. I've heard it called Rickettsial Illness by some people. It happens a lot when you're in the tropics.'

'Are you sure that's what it is?'

'Pretty sure. It's the black spot that gives it away.'

OK, so now she knew she wasn't getting headaches

and fainting for no reason. It didn't take away the aches and pains but it did explain them and in a funny way she felt reassured. 'Ricke ... what?'

'Rickettsial Illness.' James's face was glum as he poured some water into a coconut shell cup and handed it to her. 'At home they treat it with amoxicillin or some other type of antibiotic.'

'Like the pills you took for your broken ribs?' Fleur knew that he'd been in agony until he'd started taking them but that soon after that the pain had eased and he'd started to feel better. 'Are there any left?'

'I'm afraid not, Fleury.' Her dad's expression was even more woebegone. If only he hadn't used up the only medicine that would help Fleur through tick-bite fever. 'I took the last tablet the day before yesterday. The packet is empty, worse luck.'

Chapter Six

That night a storm blew in. It whipped waves into a frenzy of swirling foam as they smashed against the rocks and ripped palm fronds from their trunks and sent them crashing on to the Fisher family's shelter. Rain pelted on to the mountain top and ran in rivulets down the slopes, forming new waterfalls over sheer rocks and eroding the sandy earth. It fell so fast that the lookout fire soon hissed and died, forcing Katie to struggle down from the ledge to seek refuge in the shelter on the beach.

'At least the new roof is holding up,' she gasped as she joined the others, who stayed awake as the storm raged. She was so wet that it looked as if she'd stepped straight out of the shower.

A fork of lightning streaked across the black sky,

followed by a loud crack of thunder and then another bolt of lightning and another in quick succession. Wind howled through the trees.

'You took a big risk, coming out into the open,' James pointed out as he handed her a dry T-shirt.

Katie agreed. 'I was between a rock and a hard place – literally. Either I stayed up there and risked being blown off the mountain by a hurricane or else I made my way down here and braved the lightning.'

'Yeah – tough choice.' The next lightning bolt lit up the three faces of Fleur, Alfie and Mia. They were ashen and round-eyed with fear. Mia clung to Alfie's arm while, too weak to sit up, Fleur lay on her sleeping platform staring out towards the wild, windswept ocean. 'Anyway, we're glad you made it – aren't we, kids?'

'Yes!' Alfie, Fleur and Mia chorused.

Katie went and sat by Fleur. 'You and Alfie did a brilliant job on the roof if it can stand up to this,' she told her as she felt her forehead and pushed strands of sweat-soaked hair away from her face. 'Have you had a drink of water lately?'

With a big effort Fleur managed to nod her head. 'Dad thinks I've got tick-bite fever. I've got the rash and the aching joints and everything.'

'OK, that figures.' Katie frowned and took hold of Fleur's hand. 'Why didn't we think of it earlier?'

'And why on earth did I use up all the antibiotics?' Still guilt-stricken, James went to the doorway then darted outside to throw more wood on the fire in the

hope that it would outlast the storm. Feeble sparks rose, only to be extinguished by the lashing rain.

Katie followed him and laid a gentle hand on his shoulder. 'You weren't to know.'

'But look at her. She's burning up – God knows how high her temperature is.'

'I get it – we'd both change places with Fleur in a heartbeat. Then we'd be the ones fighting off the fever.

But that isn't going to happen, so the best we can do is make sure she drinks plenty of water and wait for it to pass.'

'*If* it passes,' James muttered. Another log on the fire raised a shower of red sparks and a sudden flare of new flames lit up their faces for a few seconds before dying back into the embers.

'Yes – *if*,' Katie had to agree. She folded her arms and turned towards the dark, stormy sea, trying not to think the worst.

Unknown to them, Alfie had crept out to join them by the fire. Overhearing every word, he turned and withdrew silently into the shelter.

'I'm scared,' Mia whimpered as yet another bolt of lightning forked through the black sky.

Alfie heard Fleur draw uneven breaths and turn painfully on to her side. 'Me too,' he admitted.

Not as scared as he had been when the storm had struck *Merlin* and the waves had swept him overboard. And not as scared as when he'd been adrift on the raft.

But Fleur being ill came a close third. *What if she doesn't get better?* he asked himself.

The family had been through a lot since they were shipwrecked – being carried ashore by the dolphins, building a fire and a shelter, finding fresh water and food. But what if the tiny, almost invisible tick that had bitten Fleur's ankle turned out to be the worst thing they'd had to face on Dolphin Island so far? Worse than hurricanes and treacherous currents, worse even than the possibility of being alone and lost in the dark, mysterious jungle? Alfie shivered then put his hands over his ears to block out the sounds of wind and rain battering the shelter and of Fleur groaning.

He lay down on his mattress and tried to sleep. All through the night, as the storm raged then died away, he measured how afraid he felt. On a scale of one to ten, if shipwreck was ten then this was eight, he decided. And if Fleur was still poorly when the sun rose tomorrow and they had no medicine for her – nothing but water and waiting – then it would be a definite nine. Nine out of ten for being scared and helpless.

And there wasn't a thing that he, eleven-year-old Alfie Fisher, could do about it.

*

If anything, as the sun rose next morning, Fleur's fever was worse. The rash had spread from her arms to her legs and chest. Her joints were so painful that she had to lie on her back without moving and with her eyes closed while the others woke up and set about their early morning chores.

'Look, Fleur.' Mia came to her with a new feather she'd found under the palm trees. It was bright golden yellow and shining in the sunlight, probably from a bird of paradise's tail. 'Open your eyes and look.'

'Sorry – I can't.' The daylight hurt Fleur too much. Her eyelids felt sticky and hot.

'It's for you anyway,' Mia insisted. She placed the prized feather on Fleur's chest and tiptoed away.

Alfie brought water and made her drink. 'Here's the bottle. I'll prop your head up with my arm. Try to swallow.'

Fleur took a gulp. The water came out too fast and some of it trickled down her chin.

'Leave her to rest,' James advised. 'Keep an eye on her while your mum and I go up to Lookout Point and rebuild the fire.'

So Alfie stayed close to base camp. He tidied the food store which was made up of fruit, nuts and fish, then covered it with palm fronds weighted down with stones. Then he took T-shirts and shorts that were wet from the storm and laid them to dry across bushes and rocks behind the shelter. As they began to steam in the heat, he shooed away monkeys sneaking up on the stash of coconuts at the door of the shelter. Next he made a handy fly swat out of a palm leaf, weaving the fronds together and testing it on an unwary wasp sunning itself on a white T-shirt. *Swish – splat!* Excellent for squishing wasps, mosquitoes and anything else with six legs and a nasty sting.

'We're up to eight knots on autopilot.' Fleur's voice drifted from the shelter. 'Moving up to full cruising speed of nine knots.'

Alfie frowned and went inside to find Fleur sitting bolt upright, staring straight ahead.

'Check the wind speed and stand by.'

'What is it?' he asked anxiously. 'Fleur, can you hear me? Are you awake?'

She ignored his questions. 'Pick up our position on

the screen. We're on autopilot. I can see rocks to starboard but it looks like we're clear ahead.'

'Fleur, you're dreaming.' Alfie's heart thumped as he knelt beside her. It was as if she could neither see nor hear him even though he leaned in towards her and spoke in a loud, persistent voice.

Fleur didn't blink. She pushed him aside and struggled to stand up. 'Quick – Mia's on the bathing platform without a life-jacket. We have to bring her down into the galley before the wind gets up.'

Luckily she was too weak to move. She suddenly stopped talking and flopped back, allowing Alfie to settle her down.

'It's OK. Everything's cool,' he murmured. 'We're not aboard *Merlin*. There was a storm. She sank, remember?'

With eyes closed, Fleur groaned at the memory. 'Oh, yes. Oh, no!'

'Yes,' he confirmed. 'We're on Dolphin Island, waiting to be rescued.'

'Dolphins.' Fleur caught at the word and echoed it dreamily. 'Here they come now. Look at that one. How cute. Do you see him, Alfie? The one with the dark eyes – that's Jazz!' Eagerly she opened her eyes and her face lit up with delight.

Alfie shook his head. He stayed quiet while, with a bright, faraway look, Fleur imagined the dolphins playing together in the bay.

'Here they come again. Jazz is super-fast. There – that's him! And here's Pearl – she's looking for you, Alfie. Where's Stormy? Mia, come quick. Stormy's missing.'

At the sound of her name, Mia stopped collecting feathers and ran into the shelter. Alfie raised a finger to his lips.

'Ah no – here he is. You can tell by his whistle. Come on into the water, Mia. Don't keep Stormy waiting.'

'It's OK – Fleur's having a dream,' Alfie whispered.

Mia shook her head. 'But she's not asleep – her eyes are open.'

'Sshh! I can see that, but she's still dreaming. You know – like sleepwalking.'

'I don't like it.' Her lip trembling, Mia hovered

uncertainly in the doorway then shot off towards the cliff. 'I'm going to tell Mum and Dad.'

'OK.' He agreed it was weird – probably something to do with Fleur's fever that made her see things that weren't actually there. Should he wake her or not?

Before he had time to decide, Fleur suddenly came to. She blinked and slowly turned her head towards him, sounding drowsy and still not quite there. 'Where am I?' she mumbled.

'In the shelter.'

'What time is it?'

'Early morning. Day 21. We've just had breakfast. Do you want some?'

'No. I want to go for a swim.' Propping herself on her elbows, she tried to swing her legs over the edge of her sleeping platform.

'No way,' Alfie protested. 'The last time you tried that, you fainted and nearly drowned.'

'But I want to.' Realizing that she was too weak to do anything, Fleur slumped forward and started to cry. She felt hot tears trickle down her cheeks. 'I want to swim in the sea with Jazz, that's all.'

'You will, when you're better,' he promised as he poured water into a bowl.

She pushed the bowl away. 'I want to do it now. Why can't I?'

'Here, drink this. You have to wait until you feel stronger.'

Fleur sighed. 'Can't I even go and see him? I won't go in the water, I swear. I'll just stay on the beach.'

'When you're better,' he insisted. Right now he couldn't see how they would even get Fleur out of the shelter and take her in the full sun to the water's edge where there was no shade and nothing to see anyway. 'Jazz isn't there,' he explained. 'The whole pod is probably miles away, deep in the ocean where there's plenty of fish and squid. They have to have breakfast, just like us.'

'But I can wait for them to come back. I can be there, ready.' Her eyes brimming with tears, she stared longingly out through the door at the white sand and the wide blue ocean.

Alfie sat cross-legged beside her. He felt more worried and helpless than ever. Then gradually an idea formed and made him realize that there was after all a way for him to help Fleur get better. *I have to make her wish come true*, he decided. *And I'm going to do it by myself.*

So he didn't say a word when Mia brought their mum and dad back – he just left the shelter and slipped away.

Out he went into the full sun, picking up the orange tent they'd salvaged from the lifeboat and preparing to carry it down the beach. He needed three straight pieces of wood – one about two metres long and the others roughly a metre and a half. He also needed some rope.

Picking out the wood he needed from the stockpile, he shouldered the rolled-up tent and the wood and set off towards George's Cave, only to find Mia trotting silently behind.

'Go back,' Alfie hissed.

'No. Why?'

'Because I want to concentrate on what I'm doing.'

'Concentrate on what? Why can't I come with you?'

He sighed. As usual Mia's pester-power won the day.

'OK, come,' he grunted.

'What are you doing?' she asked at the entrance to the cave.

George too was curious. He came off his ledge and out into the dazzling light then perched on a rock near the entrance with a quizzical look.

'I'm making a shelter for Fleur,' Alfie said with a determined glint in his eye.

'How?'

'Easy-peasy.' He stuck the longest piece of wood in the soft sand at the entrance to the cave then placed the other two to either side. Then he climbed on to the top of George's Cave, picked up a rock and started to hammer the longest pole further into the sand. He did the same with the others – six or seven heavy knocks until all three stood upright and solid. 'OK, now we have to unroll the tent.'

Once they'd laid it flat on the sand, Alfie asked Mia for the knife. 'We make three holes – one in the middle and one at each side. Then we stick the whole thing over the poles. The poles slot into the holes in the canvas – see!'

He worked quickly, asking Mia for help when it came to forming a tent-shaped roof by stretching the canvas from the pole end to the top of the cave. They pulled it taut then weighted the free end down with heavy rocks, making sure that it wouldn't blow away in the first gust of wind. Jumping down on to the beach, he took a couple of steps back to view their work. 'Cool awning, huh?'

'Very cool,' Mia agreed. 'But why are we doing this?'

'Fleur wants to watch out for Jazz and the others, but she's too sick to make it down here and stay out in the sun. Now she can sit in the shade and wait for Jazz ...'

Mia clapped her hands in glee then shot off to deliver the good news.

'... If Mum and Dad will let her,' Alfie added as he walked slowly after her.

Chapter Seven

'Hmm – maybe.' Katie wasn't sure about Alfie's latest idea. She rarely made a decision on the spur of the moment and needed time to think things through. 'It's very kind of you to be thinking about how to help Fleur get better, but taking her down to the shoreline might not be that practical.'

She stood with James, Mia and Alfie outside the base camp shelter. They talked quietly so as not to disturb Fleur, who had at last fallen asleep.

Alfie screwed up his mouth and flashed a questioning look at his dad.

'Your mum's right. What happens when the tide comes in for a start?'

Mia jumped in with an answer. 'It doesn't come up as far as George's Cave, remember.

It's always dry inside there.'

'True.' James turned to Katie. 'What do you think?'

She peered in at a peacefully sleeping Fleur. 'I don't know. Somehow it feels safer to leave Fleur where she is.'

'But you weren't here, Mum.' Alfie remembered the pleading look in Fleur's eyes when she'd begged to go down to the water. 'She was crying because she couldn't see Jazz. It was the only thing she said that made any sense.'

'What do you mean?'

'The rest was crazy stuff about being on *Merlin*, checking wind speed and cruising on autopilot.'

'The fever must have made her delirious.' James walked a little way down the beach, lost in thought. Then he stood and stared at the orange awning that Alfie and Mia had built.

'After the stuff about *Merlin* she came round a bit and seemed to know where she was. She said she wanted to go swimming with the dolphins,' Alfie went on.

'She can't do that, obviously.' For Katie, the frightening memory of Fleur fainting and being brought ashore by Jazz was still strong. 'On the other hand, if she was close to the water and the dolphins did come visiting, at least she would be able to see them.'

'I'll stay with her,' Alfie promised. 'I'll make sure she doesn't go in the water.'

Katie folded her arms and tried to see how this might work. 'Yes. Someone would always have to be there, just in case.'

'We can take it in turns,' Mia said.

'And how would we get her down there?' Practical as ever, Katie pointed out another obstacle. 'She's too weak to walk. And your dad and I can't carry her – his ribs haven't healed properly yet.'

'OK, so I've thought about that.' Alfie was ready with an answer. 'Fleur can lie on her sleeping platform and we can drag the whole thing down the beach without her having to move a muscle – like pulling her on a sledge.'

'That would be quite a weight. But it's possible,' Katie realized. 'Especially if one of us makes sure that Fleur knows what's happening and she doesn't try to move. We can use palm fronds to shade her from the sun. Then, once we've got her there, she'll have to stay in the shade, under the awning.'

'That's why we built it.' Alfie could tell that his mum was slowly coming round to the idea.

'And we'll have to wait until she wakes up before we do anything.'

'Yay!' Mia beamed then did a little dance in the soft sand. 'We can do it!'

'Can we?' Katie waited for James to rejoin them. 'Would it be the best thing for her?'

'Alfie's right,' he said as he slipped his arm around his son's shoulder. 'Fleur loves Jazz more than anything. If he can't help her get better, nothing and nobody can.'

*

Fleur woke with a start around midday. 'Watch out,' she cried in a thin, high voice. 'Rocks to starboard. Alfie, check the screens to work out a clear passage.'

Alfie and Mia had been napping while their mum and dad got lunch ready – eel steaks fried in coconut oil instead of the usual fish.

'It's OK,' Alfie told Fleur as he crouched beside her

bed. 'We're not near any rocks. We're on dry land. You're safe.'

'Oh.' She looked at him bleary-eyed. Her head throbbed and her mouth was parched. When she tried to lick her lips they felt as rough as sandpaper. 'Alfie?'

'Yes, I'm here.' Reaching for the damp cloth that Katie had left by Fleur's sleeping platform, he wiped her forehead. 'How do you feel?'

'Lousy. Can I have a drink?'

'Here.' He gave her the bottle that he'd just filled up and watched her swallow water in great gulps. 'Better?'

'Yeah, thanks.' She fell back listlessly, trying to make her eyes focus.

Alfie patted her hand. 'Listen – you know you wanted to see Jazz?'

Fleur turned her head towards him with a glimmer of eagerness in her dull eyes. Her heart ached with longing for a glimpse of his sleek shape in the clear water. 'Yes. Has he come to see me?'

'Not yet. But we've got a plan. This is what we're going to do …'

*

'Easy does it.' James was in charge of keeping Fleur comfortable as they moved her down to George's Cave. He carried a bottle of water in one hand and with the other he held a roughly woven parasol of palm fronds over her. He made sure she lay still while Alfie and Katie lifted one end of her platform, took the strain and began to heave. 'Keep your eyes closed so the sun doesn't dazzle you,' he told Fleur. 'That's right – this won't take long. We'll soon be at George's Cave. Whoa – steady!'

Dragging Fleur's bed two hundred metres across the sand was tougher than Alfie had expected. He and Katie had to walk backwards, with Mia there to guide them past any rocks that were in their way.

'Left a bit. Now straight on. More left!'

He started to sweat and grunt in the heat and his arms began to ache. 'How far is it?' he gasped at Mia.

'You're more than halfway,' she replied. 'No more rocks – it's smooth sand from now on.'

'Are you OK, Alfie? Do you need a rest?' Katie asked.

He gritted his teeth. 'No – keep going.'

They went on for what felt like for ever and every time they stepped into a dip in the sand and tilted the platform by mistake, Fleur gave a groan. Sweat ran down Alfie's face. If they didn't get there soon, he would need that rest after all. Behind him he heard the gentle lapping of waves and the sharp cries of startled sandpipers and storm petrels as they rose from the rock pools and flew away.

'Fantastic, Alfie – you're doing brilliantly.' His dad's encouragement helped him to carry on. 'Only a few more steps. Fleur, can you feel that sea breeze? Excellent. We're almost there.'

At last they reached the new awning at the entrance to George's Cave. Carefully Alfie and Katie placed Fleur's bed under it, making sure that she was facing the sea.

'How's that?' Katie asked.

'Good, thanks.' Fleur gave her mum and dad a weak smile. She saw that the sea close to the shore was bright turquoise and glittering in the sunlight. Further away, past *Merlin*'s reef, it turned to azure then melted into a heat haze that shimmered on the empty horizon. 'Still no dolphins,' she sighed.

James looked out from under the brim of his hat. 'No, it's a big, old empty ocean out there. But don't worry – the whole pod will drop by for another visit before too long.'

'Let's hope.' Katie scanned the headlands to either side of the bay and satisfied herself that all was well. 'Now who's going to stay here with Fleur and who's going to come back to base and eat some lunch?'

Mia was first off the mark. 'Me – I'll stay.'

'OK. Then in a little while you and Alfie can change places.' Katie set off up the beach with James and Alfie. 'Look after Fleur for us, Mi-mi. Don't pester her. If she's tired, let her rest.'

'Some hope,' Alfie grumbled. He couldn't imagine Mia staying silent for more than ten seconds. But then again ... He glanced over his shoulder to see Mia sitting in the shade with Fleur, quiet as a mouse. So quiet in fact that little green George had ventured out of his cave and gone to perch on Mia's shoulder. Maybe he was wrong. Maybe even Mia got how sick Fleur was – which was good in one way, Alfie thought, but a hundred per cent bad in another.

Fleur couldn't say why, but somehow she felt happier by the water and she got upset when dusk came and James tried to persuade her to come back to the shelter. 'I want to stay here in case Jazz shows up during the night,' she insisted. 'If he does, I'll be able to see him in the moonlight.'

'But there's no fire down here. It'll be cold,' James argued. 'You'll be more comfy up there with us. We can keep a better eye on you.'

'Please, Dad.' All afternoon she'd drifted in and out of sleep, still having nightmares about storms and monsters. She'd tried to eat but hadn't succeeded. She'd drunk plenty though. 'Alfie can bring his bed down here then stay and look after me. He can build a new fire.'

'Yeah – I can do that,' Alfie agreed.

James sighed then gave in, gesturing towards three macaques busily scooping crabs out of rock pools on the nearest headland. 'The fire is a good idea – it'll keep those monkeys at bay for a start. Alfie, come and get what you need. If there's any sign of trouble during the night, fetch me straight away – OK?'

So, as night fell and a pale moon sat low in the sky, Alfie got ready to spend the night at George's Cave. He brought fire from base camp by carrying a flaming branch across the sand and setting light to a small pyramid of dry wood from inside the cave. The crackling flames quickly took hold so he piled on bigger pieces of wood and soon there was a good, strong fire sending a spiral of white smoke up into the dark sky.

For a while Fleur relaxed in its warmth, but then a fresh bout of fever set in. It rolled over her like an unstoppable wave, bringing hot sweats and more nightmares, making her clench her teeth and grip the sides of the bed while a worried Alfie sat by and watched.

'Shall I fetch Dad?' he asked.

'No, Alfie – don't leave me. Go and look in George's Cave – is something horrible hiding in there?'

He stood up and did as she asked. 'Only bats,' he reported.

'Are you sure? I must have dreamed it then.'

'Dreamed what?' It was late and Alfie's eyelids

drooped. To keep himself awake he put more wood on the fire.

'It's a … creature! I see it a lot.'

'What kind of creature?' he asked fearfully. In fact, he'd prefer not to know about Fleur's bad dreams.

'Sometimes it's a gorilla, but it's got a different face – more pointy and hairy, like a wolf. Then it turns into a bear with long claws. I think it comes out of the jungle.'

'It's not real though, is it?' Alfie said. 'I mean, you're imagining it.'

Fleur sighed. 'I don't know. What if there really is something that lives deep in there that we haven't seen yet?'

'We've been here ages so how come we haven't seen it? Is it because it only comes out at night?' Though he didn't want to believe Fleur, he couldn't help shivering with fear.

'Yes. A lot of animals are nocturnal – like bats, for instance.'

'Foxes,' Alfie added. 'Hyenas and jackals. Big cats such as leopards and panthers – I expect they hunt at night.' In danger of letting his imagination run out of control, he gave himself a good shake and tried to stay calm. 'Anyway, I'm telling you – there's nothing like that in the cave, so you can relax. Try to sleep.'

It took a long time of shifting and sighing, twitching and groaning, but at last both Fleur and Alfie fell asleep. They slumbered on as the sun edged above the horizon, lighting up their pod of dolphins that circled half a mile offshore. Stars still glimmered overhead and the sea glinted in the moon's fading silvery light.

Out by *Merlin*'s reef, Jazz leaped out of the water into the calm air. Pearl and Stormy followed him – three young dolphins breaching clear of the waves, twisting their lithe bodies before they plunged out of sight. There was scarcely a ripple or a splash as they disappeared into the clear depths where they cruised amongst shoals of angelfish and stingrays, between fairytale pinnacles of pink coral, out of sight.

Chapter Eight

The sun climbed higher in the sky. A new day began.

Mia and Katie came down from the shelter with the news that Katie had discovered sugarcane growing amongst the bushes behind their camp. 'Taste it,' Mia told Alfie as she handed him a piece. It was hard and green on the outside and soft and white in the middle and was so sweet and chewy that it made your tongue stick to the roof of your mouth.

Next she offered some to Fleur. 'Taste it. It's yummy.'

Fleur shook her head. 'Maybe later.'

Katie sat down with Mia in the shade. 'Dad's got breakfast ready for you,' she told Alfie.

He said goodbye to Fleur and went on chewing as he sauntered up the beach, stooping every now and then to pick up a flat pebble suitable for skimming practice later in the day. His record so far was eight bounces on the surface of the water before the stone sank out of sight. He sorted the pebbles by size and stacked them all in a niche in a rock then sat by the campfire, drawn by the smell of smoked fish.

James greeted him with a high-five then handed him a fillet of fish on a flat clam shell that they used as a plate. 'Your mum says she wants to spend the morning with Fleury.'

'OK, cool.' Alfie replied with his mouth full.

'I'll do a shift up at Lookout Point.' James got ready to set off. 'How did Fleur do during the night?'

'The same. Bad dreams and stuff. She slept a bit but she's not eating,' he mumbled.

'Is she still waiting for Jazz to come?'

'Yes but he didn't show up, worse luck.' Alfie swallowed the last of his fish. 'So is it OK if I go exploring again?'

'Yep,' James agreed. 'You deserve some time off. But it's the same rules as before – don't risk the currents on any of the headlands. And if it looks like rain, head straight back.'

Setting off on a full stomach, Alfie had plenty of energy as he scrambled over the headland on to Turtle Beach. He scouted for more sugarcane in the bamboo copse at the edge of the cove but was disappointed when he didn't find any. Tough – the thought of sinking his teeth into more sugary sweetness made his mouth water. But there was a spiky yucca plant growing in amongst the tall bamboo. Alfie smiled as he took out his knife. He worked at the loose soil around the base of the plant to expose a long, fleshy root that he knew was good to eat. Prising it free, he cut off the leaves and stored the forked root in a safe place. He would pick it up later, on his way back to camp. Tonight his dad would cook it in boiling water then drain it and mash it up like yam or sweet potato.

Pleased with his discovery, he carried on towards Pirate Cave Beach, pausing on the headland to look ahead towards the tall spikes of rock that bordered Black Crab Cove. Maybe today, without Mia to look after, he would be able to take his time and find a way into the unexplored cove.

He was crossing Pirate Cave Beach when his day got even better. Looking out to sea to check if there was any sign of rain, he spied a lone dolphin, its dorsal fin slicing through the choppy water, heading his way. As a wave broke and tumbled in a mass of white foam, the dolphin leaped into the air to show him her pale pink belly.

'Wow – Pearl!' Alfie raced towards the water, waving his arms and yelling.

She dived down then came up again, twenty metres from the shore, greeting Alfie with friendly chirrups.

'Hi!' Without thinking, he plunged into the sea and swam out to meet her, tossed by waves and dragged sideways by a current until Pearl arrived. He was about to go under but managed to reach out just in time and grab her flipper. 'Am I glad to see you,' he yelled above the crash of the waves. He slithered on to her back and held tight to her fin as, with a quick flick of her tail, she turned and made for the headland leading into Black Crab Cove.

As long as he stayed in contact with Pearl, Alfie didn't think about the danger of swimming round the headland into the hidden cove. She forged through the deep water, avoiding rocks to either side, weaving her way through narrow channels towards the shore then holding still so that Alfie could take in his first clear sight of Black Crab Cove from the sea.

It was narrow, with long shadows cast by the rocks across a small patch of pale sand. The water swirled and foamed under dark ledges or else hit the rocks full on and threw spray high into the air. There were no trees or bushes – just bare cliffs that rose sheer out of the water to a height of twenty metres or more.

'This is cool!' Alfie liked the wildness of the scene. He leaned forward to pat Pearl who flicked her tail flukes and gave a series of friendly clicks. Then she swam slowly towards the next headland. *OK, where are we going now?* he wondered.

Straight ahead there was a high arch of rock made over millions of years by the action of the waves breaking against the shore – a natural wonder that made Alfie marvel as they passed beneath it. From here he and Pearl entered an even narrower inlet and what he saw there took his breath away.

High on the small beach, wedged between rocks was the wooden hull of an old sailing ship. It lay on its side like a beached whale, with splintered masts and gaping holes in the deck. 'Wow!' Hardly able to believe his eyes, he blinked then looked again. Yes – the wreck was real. He could make out a rusty anchor chain, a worn figurehead and the caved-in remains of the captain's cabin. 'OK, wait here,' he told Pearl, slipping from her back into the water and swimming strongly for shore. He drew breath and waded out of the water then ran towards the wreck. Scrambling up the sun-bleached hull, he peered through the nearest porthole to come face to face with a giant iguana perched on a spar of rotting wood.

Alfie recoiled in shock while the dragon-like reptile lumbered off along the pole and out of sight.

What happened here? Alfie wondered. *Who sailed this ship and how long ago?* The vessel must be hundreds of years old, built long before ships had steam engines. He could see where the mainsail and the foresail had been, though the canvas had completely rotted away. *What had life on deck been like? What dangers had the crew sailed through and had they met a sudden end trapped below deck?* One thing was for sure – the cruel sea had shown no mercy.

Fired up by curiosity, Alfie lowered himself through the porthole into the belly of the ship. *There might be skeletons of sailors down here*, he thought with a shiver – skulls with grinning jaws and hollow eye sockets, and ribs and leg bones scattered all over the place. Or old swords and pistols perhaps. Plates and tankards, knives, scraps of clothing, silver coins. But no – he searched and found nothing except spiders and cobwebs, and a big black snake coiled up at the stern end.

Alfie made a hasty exit, scrambling out into the bright daylight and making sure that Pearl still waited patiently in the shallow water. Then he sat for a while on the bleached hull, legs dangling, resting his heels against the knobbly white barnacles stuck fast to the wood.

Maybe Mia had been right about the treasure-chest in Pirate Cave, he thought. Perhaps it wasn't so fantastic after all. This old wreck could actually have been sailed by a pirate like Long John Silver, with a wooden leg and a crocodile for a pet. 'Avast, me hearties!' He would have worn a tricorne hat with a white ostrich feather and a long scarlet jacket trimmed with gold braid and buttons. The ship could have been flying the Jolly Roger flag when it went down with every man on board …

From the water Pearl made her whistling call, meaning, *Hurry up. We have to go.* At least, that's what Alfie guessed she meant when he spotted a band of inky-black clouds hanging low over the horizon.

'OK, I'm coming.' He slid down the hull and landed in soft sand. 'Wait until I tell the others about this,' he said to Pearl as he sprinted down the beach and into the water. 'It turns out we're not the first people to be shipwrecked on Dolphin Island. Those guys beat us to it by hundreds of years.'

*

He rejoined Pearl and they headed for home through a choppy sea. To Alfie, it felt as if he was riding a bucking bronco – up and down then up again, thrown about by the rough waves. He held on tight until Turtle Beach came in sight, then he pointed towards the shore. 'I have to stop here,' he murmured.

Clever Pearl felt the shift of his weight and changed course to drop him off where he wanted to be. She swam to the shoreline and let him dismount, waiting for another wave to arrive and pull her back into the water.

'Thanks. See ya!' Alfie called as she disappeared in the white foam.

She opened her mouth and gave a clicking, chirping answer. Then she spouted water from her blowhole, turned tail and swam away.

Happily Alfie ran up the beach to collect the yucca root. He tucked it under his arm then climbed the headland, spotting Mia still chatting with Fleur under the bright orange awning outside George's Cave. 'Hey, you two – you're not going to believe this!' he yelled.

Eagerly he crossed the beach and joined them. 'I've seen an old wreck. Mia, you'll never guess where.'

Mia threw aside the miniature shell necklace that she'd been making for Monkey. She jumped up and ran to meet Alfie. 'Where?'

'Past Black Crab Cove. I'm talking about a Robinson Crusoe sailing ship type of thing – made of wood, with a carved figurehead and masts. I searched for treasure but there wasn't any. It was still cool though.' The words tumbled out of Alfie's mouth but he managed to hold back the part of his adventure involving Pearl because he thought it wouldn't be fair on Fleur. After all, she was still waiting longingly for a first glimpse of her precious Jazz. 'I reckon the ship sank in a storm with all men on board.'

'It does sound cool.' Fleur was envious. Right now it was too hard even to lift her head from her pillow, let alone set off on a major explore. She couldn't deny it – it was scary to feel this weak and helpless. 'Did the ship have a name?'

'Not one that I could see. There's only a hulk left and even that's rotting away.'

'I know – let's call it *The Dolphin*,' Mia's eyes shone with excitement. 'I read the letters on the side.'

'OK, *Dolphin*,' Alfie agreed. 'Anyhow, I climbed in through one of the portholes to look for useful stuff inside the hull, but all I found was cobwebs, a big old iguana and a black snake.'

'I wish I could've been there,' Fleur said with a sigh. 'Did you bring back any planks of wood for the fire?'

Alfie frowned. 'It was kind of hard to get to,' he said cagily. 'You have to climb some cliffs.'

'OK, so you couldn't carry anything.' This made sense to Fleur, who seemed to lose interest in Alfie's adventure. 'I've been waiting and waiting all night and all day for Jazz, but no luck so far. Mia said she spotted the pod around noon.'

'I did,' Mia insisted. 'Cross my heart I saw them.'

'But they were miles away, out on the horizon.' Fleur's pale face was frowning and sad as she gazed out at the gathering clouds. 'None of them came to visit us. And they won't for a while – not if there's a storm.'

Alfie pursed his lips then he changed the subject. 'I found yucca,' he said as he handed the root over to Mia. 'Take this up to Dad. Ask him to cook it for our tea.'

So Mia grabbed Monkey and ran up the beach with the yucca, leaving Alfie to carry on chatting to Fleur about the discovery of the wreck.

'So anyway, people were here before us, back in the olden days. Maybe we're on an old trade route between, say, the Solomon Isles and Europe but the ship got blown off course, just like *Merlin* did. Only, they didn't have any network systems on board with echo-sounders and electric compasses and radar. Back then they had to navigate by the stars and old-fashioned charts drawn on parchment ...'

Alfie paused and looked at Fleur, who had drifted off to sleep. 'OK, I'm a geek,' he muttered to himself with a wry smile. Then he glanced up the beach at their dad peeling and cutting up the yucca, just in time to see Mia heading off towards Turtle Beach. *Oh, no*, he thought and his stomach lurched. *I know what she's up to – she's snuck away to find the old hulk without telling anyone.*

Yep, that was definitely it. He could tell by the way Mia was scurrying off, head down, scampering over the headland on to Turtle Beach without looking back. And it was partly his fault because he'd been so excited about finding the wreck and he'd told her exactly where it was.

'She's crazy. Doesn't she know it's time to eat and anyway there's going to be a storm?' he muttered. He spoke quietly so as not to wake Fleur and was caught between running up the beach to tell their dad what was happening or making a beeline towards the headland and catching up with Mia. She was already over the rocks and vanishing down the far side. Best to go after her and bring her back, he decided.

So he left Fleur to sleep and followed Mia as fast as he could, over the headland on to Turtle Beach where he saw that she still had a good lead on him and had only begun to slow down when she came to the rocks at the far side of the bay.

'Come back!' he yelled, cupping his hands to his lips. His voice didn't carry over the sound of the waves crashing on to the shore and now he was seriously worried that he wouldn't catch up with her before the storm hit the island. There she was – a small, sunburned figure in turquoise swimmie and a home-made straw hat, scrambling over the headland out of sight.

Alfie put on a spurt. He sprinted as hard as he could, feeling the first splashes of cold rain on his face. Mia was only six and he was eleven – surely his long legs would allow him to gain on her and stop her as she crossed Pirate Cave Beach, before she reached the perilous rocks of Black Crab Cove?

Sure enough, he climbed the headland and saw that the gap between them was less. 'Mia!' he yelled again and this time she stopped and turned around. 'Come back!'

Mia frowned back at him. It wasn't fair – all she wanted to do was to see the old ship and now here was Alfie trying to stop her. As she stood and wondered whether or not to ignore him, a gust of strong wind blew her hat off and bowled it up the beach towards Pirate Cave. She gave chase but the wind kept the hat a few metres ahead of her until at last she darted forward and trapped it with her foot.

'I said, come back!' When he finally caught up with her, Alfie was really mad. 'You can't just run off without telling anyone – it's against the rules.'

'I just wanted … I mean, I didn't think … OK, I shouldn't have.' Mia ran out of feeble excuses and she hung her head. 'Sorry, Alfie.'

'Now look.' He pointed out to sea at the approaching storm. 'It's already raining. That's a tornado out there and it's heading this way. We'll never get back home in time.'

It was true – the wind had whipped the bank of clouds into a dark funnel that was racing across the sea straight at them. The sun had vanished and the sea looked black.

'We'll have to take shelter in Pirate Cave,' Alfie decided.

This was easier said than done. As the wind grew stronger, it battered against Mia's slight frame, tipping her off balance so that her hat was whisked from under her foot. It whirled high into the air. 'Oh no!' she wailed.

Off it went. The bright feathers that decorated it were torn free and spiralled off separately from the battered hat.

'Leave it.' Alfie knew that the hat was lost and there was no time to lose – they had to reach safety before the full force of the tornado hit land. So he took hold of Mia's hand and dragged her towards the cave, shielding his face from the whirling, gritty sand that was whipped up by the wind. The entrance wasn't far away – he made out the pinnacles of rock to each side and the boulder partly blocking their way. But he wasn't sure they could make it. 'Don't let go of my hand,' he told Mia as he tried to shield her from the full force of the howling wind and rain.

'I can't see,' she cried. 'I've got sand in my eyes.'

'Keep them closed. Hang on to me.'

They had to cling to one another and inch their way forward, heads bowed. Rain lashed down on to their shoulders and backs as at last they reached the cave.

'You first.' Alfie guided Mia under the boulder then gave time to allow her to crawl through the narrow gap. 'You OK?'

'Yes,' she called, her voice muffled and choked with tears.

'OK, don't move. I'm on my way.' There was just enough room for him to wriggle through and as he felt flat, dry pebbles on the far side, he let out a loud sigh of relief. 'Cool – we made it. Don't cry. Everything's OK.'

Outside, the tornado hit full force. It felled palm

trees along the shoreline then swept on up the cliffs, uprooting bushes and sending the animals of Dolphin Island scurrying for safety into the depths of the jungle.

Mia cowered against the boulder that blocked the cave entrance. There was no rain in here and no wind, but her heart was pounding nevertheless. She stared through the gloom at Alfie with wide, round eyes.

They crouched inside the cave and waited for the storm to blow itself out.

'What about Fleur?' Mia whimpered as the wind wailed and the rain battered the rocks. 'Will she be OK?'

He thought of George's Cave and the orange awning that sheltered Fleur, of their sister too sick and weak to move out of the path of the tornado. 'Let's hope so,' he said through gritted teeth. 'But honestly I have no idea.'

Chapter Nine

When James felt the first strong gusts of wind blow off the sea, he glanced down the beach. *Uh-oh*, he thought, *those clouds don't bode well*. He lifted his pan of boiling yucca off the fire then hurried to join Fleur at the entrance to George's Cave.

'Where are Alfie and Mia?' he asked her with a worried frown.

Fleur opened her eyes and stared blankly back. 'I have to do my History revision,' she mumbled. 'It's my exam tomorrow.'

James crouched beside her bed. The clouds heading towards the island didn't look good and neither did Fleur. Her face was flushed and the rash on her arms and legs had grown redder. She didn't seem to have a clue where she was.

Right now he ought to make her his priority. But first he took a quick look around – up at Katie at Lookout Point, busily stoking the fire, then south along the beach towards Turtle Beach. There were two fresh sets of footprints leading towards the headland but no sign of the missing pair.

'OK, Fleury, can you hear me?'

She gave him the same empty look as before and slurred her response. 'I've learned most of the stuff about the First World War but I haven't started the Second World War yet. My teacher says we have to do both.'

'I'm going to try and move you inside the cave,' he decided. 'I can tell by the direction of the wind that the storm will hit us full on so we can't risk leaving you out in the open.' Taking hold of the top end of Fleur's bed and tilting it upwards, he prepared to heave. 'Ready?'

Fleur groaned and closed her eyes as she felt her bed shift. Someone was talking to her but she couldn't make sense of what he was saying.

'Hold on,' James warned. He pulled with all his

might, gritting his teeth and doing his best to ignore the nagging pain in his ribs. 'We'll soon have you safe and dry.'

Centimetre by centimetre he lugged Fleur's bed into the cave. He dragged it to one side, away from the exposed entrance, then went out again and quickly yanked the awning poles out of the sand. He dragged the whole thing – canvas and poles – inside the cave. 'OK, Fleury, I'm going to make a windbreak for you. With luck it'll keep out most of the wind and rain.'

He worked quickly to form a canvas barrier, desperately trying to work out what to do next. 'I don't know if it's best to stay here with you or to go after Mia and Alfie.'

As he spoke, rain started to fall, slowly at first but soon turning into a downpour and leaving him no time to work out a proper plan. 'OK, I'm not happy about leaving you by yourself but I have no choice – I need to go and look for the others,' he decided. 'Don't worry – you'll be safe here.'

'OK, Dad – see you,' she said, suddenly bright and cheerful, as if he'd said he was popping out to the shop for a carton of milk. Her cheeks blazed with a feverish flush as she tried to sit up and look around.

Holding his breath, he bent over her and stroked her forehead, easing her back on to her pillow before he left. 'Don't move. Take it easy. I won't be long.'

He pulled up one corner of the windbreak and crawled out on to the sand. The wind was already smoothing out Alfie and Mia's footprints and the flat bank of black clouds had started to form a funnel shape on the horizon. It could only mean one thing – a tornado was on its way. Who knew when it would hit and what damage it would do? With his heart in his mouth, James said goodbye to Fleur then left George's Cave and sprinted for the headland.

Inside the cave, trapped inside her fevered cocoon, Fleur drifted through events from the Second World War. She'd recited out loud the dates when German bombs had started to fall on London and when British and American soldiers had landed on the beaches of Normandy, before a sudden, savage gust of wind tore down the orange barricade and let in the torrential rain. As the canvas collapsed and fell on top of her, she clawed at it with her hands, wrenching it from her face and pushing it aside. Seemingly revived by the cold rain, she caught a glimpse of the dark storm hitting the shore in a flurry of foam and spray. She took a deep breath and gathered enough strength to roll from her bed then crawl slowly towards the entrance where she came to a halt and cried out.

For there, close to the shore, was a white boat tossed like a cork in the raging, foaming water – an offshore cruising yacht like *Merlin*, with its sails furled and relying on its engine to struggle towards land.

It couldn't be true. It was another dream, a nightmare. On her knees in the entrance to George's Cave, Fleur felt the rain on her face and saw the tornado whirl its way towards shore. Was that part of the nightmare too? She raised a hand to touch her wet, cold cheek and looked out in wonder.

It was definitely there – a yacht, just visible through the rain, was heading for the rocks where *Merlin* had come to grief. Its navigation lights to bow and stern were flashing and she shuddered as she saw one of the metal masts buckle and break under the twisting force of the wind. It smashed down on to the cabin as, with a flash of white, the hull tilted clear of the water. Fleur held her breath until the boat bobbed upright again, lights still flashing, and surging on towards the black rocks.

It was *Merlin* all over again. It was a dream, she decided – the wreck was playing out a second time, only now Fleur was an outsider looking on. But no – she could see two sailors in orange life-jackets, up on deck, clinging to the remains of the mast. She gasped and cried out in terror as one let go and crawled towards the guard wire to starboard, held on to it for dear life and wrenched the lifeboat free of its bracket. The other still clung to the mast.

The boat was by now so close to the reef where *Merlin* had gone down that Fleur couldn't bear to look. She closed her eyes then forced herself to open them again and saw everything that happened next in slow motion, like a clip from a silent movie.

The boat hit the reef and shuddered to a halt. There was no crunch of hull against rock, no cries of fright, no words – only the almighty roar and crash of waves. As the boat toppled on to its side, one of the sailors inflated the lifeboat and flung it into the water. Seconds later, both had leaped from their holed vessel into the inflatable. A pink distress flare shot high into the dark sky leaving a plume of smoke.

As if paralysed, Fleur stared at the scene and saw that it was real. Another storm, another shipwreck. Two sailors. A lifeboat … a lifeboat! A flare! Breaking free from her stupor, she crawled out of the cave. She tried to stand but collapsed on to one knee.

A gap was opening up between the lifeboat and the stricken yacht, which meant that the sailors had started the outboard motor and intended to steer out to sea.

'This way!' Fleur yelled. 'Come back – this way!' Though the wind had started to die down, she couldn't be heard.

Without looking over their shoulders, the men sailed away from the treacherous coastline out into the ocean. Their stricken boat shifted on the rocks and settled. The next mountainous wave lifted it almost free then receded. The boat shifted again, wallowing lower in the water so that only a small part of the deck was visible.

'Come back,' Fleur murmured to the shipwrecked sailors.

A second flare lit up the stormy sky. Oblivious of Fleur and her family stranded on Dolphin Island, the two sailors headed north towards the next inhabited island and rescue.

*

'I did – I swear I saw it!' Why wouldn't Alfie and Mia believe her? Fleur knelt in the entrance to George's Cave.

'You're shivering,' Alfie told her. He wrapped the bulky orange canvas around her shoulders then persuaded her to crawl back inside and sit on her bed.

'There was a boat. It ran aground on *Merlin*'s rock,' she said again.

'Well, it's not there now.' The tornado had passed and the sea was calm. Fleur must have been having one of her nightmares. 'Sit down. Let's wait here for Mum and Dad.'

Mia sat beside Fleur and tried to sniff back her tears.

124

'Dad nearly got blown away,' she confessed miserably. 'It was my fault. I wanted to see the pirates' ship. Alfie followed me then Dad had to come and find us. He nearly didn't make it to Pirate Cave.'

'But he did and we're all OK.' Alfie tried to look on the bright side. He expected there'd be a new rule after this latest crisis – at least if their mum had anything to do with it. Something along the lines of 'Never Ever Let Mia out of Your Sight, Not for a Single Second'.

'I saw a boat,' Fleur insisted. 'A cruising yacht just like *Merlin*, with a lifeboat and flares.'

'So where is it then?' Alfie looked out towards the reef and saw nothing. He didn't blame Fleur for having bad dreams about being thrown overboard – he had them himself. 'Anyway, Dad went to fetch Mum down from Lookout Point. He wants to get us back together, all in one place for tonight at least.'

Fleur sighed and shook her muddled, aching head. 'Tell him I want to stay here and wait for Jazz.'

'He already knows that.' Alfie rearranged the canvas around Fleur to keep her warm. 'But it turns out the awning was no good during the storm. It wasn't strong enough. So it'll be safer for you to stay with us in the shelter from now on.'

'I don't care about being safe.' Fleur felt her stomach twist into tight knots. 'What if Jazz comes and I'm not here? He'll think I don't want to swim with him any more and he'll go away. I'll never see him again.'

'Yes, you will.' Alfie didn't blame Fleur for being afraid of this either. Being able to swim with Pearl, Stormy and Jazz was the one thing that boosted their spirits and gave them hope. 'I know how much you need to see him. But, don't worry – I bet you he knows you're sick.'

'How does he?' Mia wondered.

'He just does. Dolphins know these things. I reckon Jazz will hang around until you get better.'

Listening to their voices, Fleur closed her eyes. Had there truly been a boat or had she dreamed it? Had there been a tornado? Was Jazz even real?

Yes, she thought, as James and Katie came down the beach. Jazz, with his high-low call, his aerial acrobatics and his sweet cuddles, was the only thing she was sure of. He was out there in the clear ocean waiting for her and one day soon she would be strong again. The pink sun would rise above the glittering horizon and turn to gold. They would swim together once more.

Chapter Ten

On Dolphin Island, storm was always followed by calm.

Fleur lay perfectly still on her bed and gazed out at the dawn of Day 23 – at first a glimmer on the dark horizon then a glow then a dazzle of golden light. Soon the sky turned cloudless blue.

'Are you awake?' Alfie asked when he heard her sigh.

'Yes.'

'Did you sleep?'

'A bit.' Keeping her eyes fixed on the ocean, Fleur hid the truth. In fact, every time she'd closed her eyes in the dark shelter, she'd seen flashing images of shipwreck – an upturned hull, two desperate sailors in orange life-jackets, a pink flare shooting up into blackness. 'Alfie ...' she whispered after a while. 'There really was a boat.'

'When?'

'Yesterday, during the storm.'

'So why can't we see the wreck?' Deciding it was time to get up, Alfie stood and stretched.

'I don't know. But honestly, I did see it. There were two men in a lifeboat during the tornado – they set off flares.'

He shook his head. 'How come I didn't see any flares? And for that matter, neither did anybody else.'

Though her head pounded, Fleur refused to give in. 'They sailed off, out to sea. You never know – maybe someone saw the flares and will come looking for them and for us too.'

'OK, Fleur – maybe they will.' Seeing that it was pointless to argue, Alfie walked out on to the beach and began to stoke the fire with fresh wood. He wafted smoke from his face then picked up two canisters, ready to make a trek up to the waterfall to collect fresh water.

I'm right, Fleur thought. *There was a boat. There were two men.* Who knows, they might have glanced back towards Dolphin Island as the storm had eased –

looked and seen smoke from the fire on Lookout Point then realized that there were people stranded here. Who knows, who knows ...?

*

Alfie climbed the cliff. Usually he loved early mornings on the island, before the sun got too hot. It was a time when he could pause and notice white herons down on the shoreline, digging with their long beaks in the wet sand for worms. He might even look up and spot a bird of paradise in the trees at the edge of the jungle, doing his display dance along a branch, jigging and shaking his splendid train of bright yellow feathers in the sunlight.

Today, though, Alfie was lost in thought, worrying about Fleur. She'd been sick for three days and didn't seem to be getting any better. Last night he'd overheard their mum and dad talking by the campfire, when they'd thought everyone was asleep.

'I'd better be heading off.' Katie had been preparing for her usual night shift at Lookout Point. 'Keep an eye on Fleur – make sure she doesn't do anything crazy.'

'Like trying to get back to George's Cave?' James had murmured.

'Yes. No way is she strong enough, but she probably doesn't realize that.'

'So she might try to struggle down there in the middle of the night – yeah, I hear you.' For a while, James and Katie had held an anxious silence.

'I wish we still had those antibiotics.' It had been James who had spoken again, just as Katie had sighed and got up to leave. 'I shouldn't have used them all. They would've cured Fleury of this tick-bite fever, no problem.'

'Don't beat yourself up,' Katie had told him. 'We weren't to know she'd get bitten and develop a fever.'

Wide awake and stiff with worry, Alfie had listened to every word they'd said.

'It might take longer, but she *can* get better without antibiotics,' Katie had insisted.

'Maybe.' James hadn't sounded convinced.

'Yes, she can. You'll see – after two or three weeks, Fleur will be back to her old self.'

Two to three whole weeks! When Alfie had heard

this, he'd shuddered to himself.

'Maybe,' James had said again as Katie left.

Or maybe not. Alfie had stayed still, pretending to be asleep as his dad had come into the shelter and climbed into his hammock. And what then? What if Fleur stayed sick and didn't eat? She was already pretty thin – she might waste away and actually starve. Or the infection might get even worse – her temperature could shoot up way above forty degrees and they wouldn't have any way of bringing it back down. Alfie knew that would be really bad news.

That was why he was awake at the crack of dawn, having his whispered conversation with Fleur, and why he didn't take any notice this morning of the wildlife teeming on the cliff face and by the waterfall, where he stooped to fill the first canister.

'Alfie – look!' Katie ran down the slope from Lookout Point, waving her arm wildly towards the shore.

He stood up and followed the direction of her pointing finger. What was she on about? The beach was empty and smooth; the tide was ebbing gently.

A breathless Katie reached him. 'Fleur was right after all – out on the reef, look!'

Alfie raised his gaze to take in the curve of black rocks emerging from the sea half a mile from shore. There, stuck fast, was the holed hull of a cruising yacht.

'See!' Katie beamed. 'The whole thing was hidden below the waterline last night at high tide – that's why we didn't believe her.'

He nodded and grinned back. 'Everything she said – the wreck, the lifeboat, the flares – they really happened.'

'It looks like it.' His mum took the lead, hurrying down the cliff to tell the others.

They found James cooking breakfast and Mia sitting in the shelter beside Fleur, quietly showing her some new green feathers she'd found in the bushes.

'Guess what.' Hurriedly Alfie delivered the amazing news. 'Fleur, you didn't dream it – there *is* a wreck – right where *Merlin* ran aground before she sank.'

'I knew it!' Fleur tried in vain to sit up.

Alarmed, Alfie eased her back down. 'Someone,

help me get the bed out into the open so Fleur can see for herself.'

Quickly Katie stepped in and together they dragged the bed from the shelter. 'You were right,' Alfie confirmed. 'There it is – right there on the reef.'

*

It took less than five minutes for the family to decide what to do next.

'It's obvious – we have to get out there and take a closer look.' Alfie was the first to say what everyone was thinking once they'd taken it in turns to drag Fleur's bed down to the water's edge and they gathered there for a closer look at the wreck.

'Before the tide turns,' his dad agreed. 'Come high tide, she'll disappear under the waves again and there'll be no chance to take off any useful items. The way I look at it is – she's pretty unstable so she might not stay where she is for much longer. This might be the only opportunity we get.'

'Now don't we all wish we'd built ourselves a new raft?' Katie regretted not putting this to the top of their list, above fire watching, food gathering and beachcombing.

'We could have rowed out there and brought back everything we could lay our hands on. As it is, we'll have to swim out and fetch just the small stuff.'

'I'll go!' Alfie was the first to volunteer. Excitement buzzed through him and he forgot his fear of the waves and currents.

'Me too – I'll go!' Mia echoed.

Fleur was silent. Her lips trembled and tears blurred her view of the wrecked boat, wedged between two rocks, its keel clear of the water. She saw that waves lapped at it and made it rock unsteadily.

'No, Mia – you're too little. But whoever swims out there had better be quick,' James noted. 'I reckon we've only got an hour or so before the tide turns.'

'But it's risky.' Taking a deep breath, Katie weighed up the pros and cons. 'We can't tell from here how safe it is. Maybe it'd be better just to go out there and pick up whatever bits of flotsam we can without venturing on board.'

'I can see a lifebuoy – it's hanging over the guardrail.' Mia dashed into the waves and had to be held back by James.

He brought her firmly back to dry land. 'What do we do?' he asked Katie.

As they stood uncertainly on the shore, it was the dolphins who solved the dilemma as usual. As if with a sixth sense, the whole pod showed up without warning. They appeared just when they were needed, swimming calmly from far out to sea towards the island then circling the new wreck before one lone dolphin split off from the rest and came close to the water's edge.

'Hey!' Alfie's eyes lit up as Pearl swam near and clapped her jaws in greeting.

The other members of the pod kept their distance.

'Look – she wants *me* to go with her,' Alfie told James and Katie proudly. He waded eagerly into the water. 'It's OK – she knows what she's doing.'

From her bed on the shoreline, Fleur watched with an aching heart. If only that could be Jazz carrying her out to the wreck instead of Pearl with Alfie. She said Jazz's name out loud, sighing loudly and allowing the tears to fall.

Without any more protests, Mia gave up her

demands. She sat down in the sand beside Fleur and held her hand.

Pearl waited patiently for a decision to be made.

'What do you think – do we let him go?' Katie said to James, who frowned then nodded.

'Yeah!' Overjoyed, Alfie flung himself into the water. He didn't look back as he clambered astride Pearl and felt her turn then surge at speed straight towards the reef. They joined Jazz and Stormy and the rest of the pod circling the wreck, swimming calmly between rocks without any of their usual fun and games. Alfie too grew serious.

'OK, Pearl – we have to get as close as we can,' he decided as he hung on to her fin and felt her twist and turn beneath him as she approached the wreck. He saw the lifebuoy hanging over the guardrail and reached out to grab it. 'Missed!' he grunted as at the last second the hull tilted away from him. Instead, he scooped up a useful length of rope dangling from the deck, yanked it free then coiled it and hung it from his shoulder. As he did so, he made out a name on the prow and said it out loud – 'Kestrel'.

137

It was a beautiful name for a once beautiful sailing boat that had skimmed gracefully through the sparkling ocean waves. Now she was marooned on the reef with a wide gash in her side. She would never sail again.

'OK, Pearl, wish me luck – I'm going to take a closer look.' Holding his breath, Alfie tipped sideways into the water, lunged towards the dangling lifebuoy and

this time managed to catch hold of it, using it to haul himself up on to the boat.

Back on shore, his mum and dad, Mia and Fleur watched him climb aboard, circled by a watchful pod.

'Please be careful,' Katie murmured, her fingers tightly crossed.

Alfie slithered on his belly across the sloping

wooden deck towards an open hatch. He reached the edge and peered into an L-shaped galley that was almost submerged. Seawater washed around what was left of a cooker that had become disconnected from its gas canister, and it lapped against a fridge whose door had been wrenched from its hinges. There were several large, airtight plastic jars bobbing on the surface – probably containing precious food supplies. Reaching in, he managed to lift two of them out of the galley. One was labelled *Flour*, the other *Rice*.

Cool. But how to carry them back, he wondered as he glanced at the rest of the family on shore. OK, this was where the salvaged rope would come in handy. Bracing himself against the guardrail, he uncoiled the rope and tied it securely around the two containers. He was happy with the result – once he was back in the water with Pearl, he could trail the jars behind them on the journey back to shore. Now, what else?

Tying one end of the rope securely to the guardrail, he made his slow way from the galley to the nearest cabin and once more peered through a hatch. Here he saw wet paperbacks and magazines floating on the surface in amongst sodden pillows and cushions, assorted shirts, shorts and a blue baseball cap. These were harder to get hold of than the food jars because each time he reached for them the boat would tilt and the seawater would wash them out of reach. Managing at last to grab a shirt and a pair of shorts, plus the cap, he pulled the shorts over his swimming trunks then struggled into the shirt and jammed the cap on his head. What next?

Of course – the first-aid box. Every seaworthy sailing vessel had one and it was usually kept in the main cabin to the aft of the boat. Why hadn't he thought of this earlier? If his dad was right and the tide was on the turn, he was fast running out of time.

A first-aid box would contain sticking plasters and antiseptic cream to keep cuts clean, tweezers to pull out thorns and antibiotics to cure infections. Of course – pills for Fleur! Alfie could have kicked himself for not making a beeline straight for the captain's cabin.

And now the waves were definitely rising higher, slapping against the upturned hull and making it rock more violently as he slid on his belly towards the cabin.

Pearl and the other dolphins swam close to *Kestrel*, rising out of the water, flapping their flippers against their sides and clicking loudly to grab Alfie's attention.

'OK, I'm on my way – this won't take a second.' Alfie was determined to find the boat's first-aid box. Nothing else mattered – not Pearl's warning whistle or James and Katie's frantic signals from shore.

He reached the cabin and tugged at the flimsy insect screen across the entrance. Managing to pull it free, he flung it into the water. In the cabin, the sea level had risen high enough to submerge many of the screens that *Kestrel*'s sailors had relied on to chart their course. During the violent storm, the captain's chair had been wrenched from the brackets that anchored it to the deck and it had smashed against another electrical console, partly blocking Alfie's way.

Pearl whistled again and once more Alfie ignored her. He remembered that Merlin's first-aid box had been stored on a high shelf behind the captain's seat so he wriggled into the cabin and felt for a shelf. He found one and ran his fingers along its length, dislodging a torch and a camera. Both fell into the water and sank.

142

But there was no first-aid box.

Strong waves hit the boat and she rocked. Alfie was thrown backwards out of the cabin and flung against the guardrail close to where he'd tied the food canisters. He came face to face with Pearl, who rose out of the sea clicking louder and faster than before. This was it – he had to leave now, right this second.

So Alfie quickly grabbed the rope with the food jars attached and jumped. Pearl was there, waiting. As the waves crashed against the rocks and sent spray high over their heads, Alfie hit the water and immediately felt Pearl's snout at his heels. He braced his legs and she shoved him hard away from *Kestrel*, propelling him through the water at high speed until they were clear of the reef. Then she slowed down and gave him time to clamber on to her back. Together they headed for shore.

Mia ran in waist-deep to meet them. She grabbed the rope that trailed the canisters then he lowered himself from Pearl's back. He stroked her before she left. 'Thanks,' he whispered.

His special dolphin had brought him back safe from

the wreck with rice and flour, and with extra clothes. It wasn't much, but it was something.

From her bed at the water's edge, Fleur watched Alfie stroke Pearl. She saw Stormy break away from the pod and swim to say a jaunty hello to Mia, turning on to his back for his white belly to be tickled. And – at long last – here was Jazz, swimming as close as he could, greeting Fleur with his signature whistle.

'Hey,' she said with a loud sigh, reaching out but feeling too weak to move from her bed.

He let the incoming tide lift him and buoy him up, gazing at her with his dark-rimmed eyes. Another wave came and broke over him. A crescent of white foam ran up the beach and reached Fleur.

High-low, high-low – Jazz gave a gentle farewell. Something was wrong with Fleur, something he could do nothing about. So he turned and followed Pearl and Stormy past the reef where *Kestrel* was battered by breaking waves. He swam slowly and sadly out to sea.

Chapter Eleven

'You did a good job,' James told Alfie as he opened the rice and flour jars to examine the contents. 'It's good news – we can have rice with our fish tonight.'

Meanwhile Alfie took off the cap, shirt and shorts and handed them to his mum. 'They're adult size. I reckon these will fit you and Dad.'

'Why so serious?' Katie asked.

'I wanted to find the first-aid box,' he admitted quietly.

She spread the new clothes across a bush to dry. 'What did you say?'

Alfie glanced at Fleur lying on her bed inside the shelter. Her eyes were closed but she was twitchy and restless – maybe having another bad dream. He saw clearly that he'd messed up. He'd missed the chance to make a proper search for the medicine that would make her better. He'd let her down. 'Nothing. It doesn't matter,' he muttered to his mum.

'I was worried about you.' The sun had bleached Katie's pink shirt almost white and the bottoms of her cut-off jeans had started to fray. Strands of fair hair blew across her tanned cheeks and she looked at him thoughtfully.

'I was OK,' he insisted. 'Pearl was keeping watch. She let me know when it was time to come back.'

'Yes, she sure did. And I'm glad Fleur got a glimpse of Jazz at last. She's been waiting for so long.'

Alfie felt a lump in his throat. He didn't feel like talking any more so he walked back down the beach and sat for a while on the headland, watching the sea rise around the rocks where *Kestrel* had run aground.

Next time, he thought. *Next time, when the tide goes out, I'll try again.*

The waves broke over the damaged hull. They rolled into the cabins and the galley and sucked out again – endlessly in and out until, without warning, they tipped the vessel clear of the deadly reef. She drifted free.

'Dad! Mum!' Alfie jumped up and yelled up the beach.

They came to the door of the shelter for a last sight of *Kestrel*, with only the gleaming tip of her curved keel visible above the rolling waves.

Alfie held his breath and watched her disappear. Gone without a trace, sinking down among the coral reefs, coming to rest among shoals of silversides and striped parrotfish.

There would be no next time, he realized. There'd only been one chance and he'd missed it.

*

He came – I saw him! Drifting in and out of sleep in the midday heat, Fleur remembered the moment when Jazz had swum to the shore. He'd approached quietly, with none of his usual show-off tricks – no tail-walking or flapping his flippers, no leaping clear of the water with an acrobatic twist. Just slow and gentle, gazing at her with his beautiful, dark-rimmed eyes.

She remembered the light, cool feel of sea spray on her face and skin. 'He came,' she murmured.

There was no one to hear. James was keeping the

fire going up at Lookout Point. Katie was on Turtle Beach cutting down bamboo for a new raft that she'd set her mind on building, while Alfie and Mia walked the shoreline to pick up any salvage from poor *Kestrel* that might have drifted ashore on the latest high tide.

Fleur opened her eyes and stared up at the roughly thatched ceiling. Insects buzzed in the fierce midday heat and a cloud of small white butterflies flitted past the entrance. Her limbs felt heavy; sweat trickled from her forehead.

She closed her eyes and pictured Jazz swimming in the clear ocean, miles from the shore. He cut through dazzling waves then arched his back and disappeared from sight, diving down into the depths with a flick of his tail flukes. He blew a million playful bubbles, silently gliding underwater then surging back to the surface to breathe. She saw him again and thrilled to his speed, his smoothness. Jazz, her soulmate, graceful and fast in the cool green ocean – swimming free.

*

Mia and Alfie's best find that afternoon was the insect screen that Alfie had wrenched from the doorway into

Kestrel's main cabin. The flimsy frame had floated ashore and been left high and dry on Echo Cave Beach as the tide turned once more. The gauze that kept out mosquitoes was still intact.

'Wowser!' Mia seized one end while Alfie held the other, ready to carry it back to base in triumph. 'This is so cool.'

Alfie couldn't help smiling. Mia had claimed the baseball cap that he'd salvaged from the wreck and though it was much too big she insisted on wearing it. The peak came down over her eyebrows and shaded the whole of her freckled face. 'Yep – cool,' he agreed.

It was a fair walk back over the headland to base camp but the screen was light and so they made their way easily across the sand on to the rocks, where they rested for a while and Alfie emptied his pockets for them to inspect the rest of their haul. There was a spatula and two folded paper plates from *Kestrel*'s galley kitchen for a start, plus a man's waterproof watch. Mia had spotted it gleaming silver in amongst a tangle of dark brown seaweed and pounced on it with delight.

'It's not digital, it's analogue,' Alfie had pronounced as he watched the second hand move slowly around the dial. 'Lucky us – it still works.'

Then they'd come across more rope and a section of *Kestrel*'s metal boarding ladder that they decided to store in Echo Cave – Alfie thought this was the second best discovery after the insect screen and was determined to come back and collect it later that day.

'OK – ready?' he asked Mia, who was trying to adjust her cap's Velcro fastening. It was no good – when she set the cap back on her head, it still came down over her eyes and she had to flip the peak up so that she could see where she was going. 'Let's go.'

They picked up their haul and set off again and soon came down from the rocks on to their own beach where they headed straight for the shelter, eager to show Fleur what they'd found.

Fleur hadn't moved from her bed. She lay with her eyes open but didn't react when Mia rushed in ahead of Alfie. Instead, she stared up at the roof with a glazed look.

'We found loads of stuff from *Kestrel*,' Mia declared.

'Alfie says we can go back again and look for more after we've had lunch.'

'I went swimming with Jazz,' Fleur said dreamily. 'The water was cool and clear as anything.'

Mia shot Alfie a worried look. He frowned and shook his head.

'It was just Jazz and me, no one else,' Fleur went on. 'He took me miles and miles out to sea.'

'Look – we found this.' Mia held up the watch.

'Miles and miles,' Fleur said again as she stared without seeing at the roof.

Mia put the watch to Fleur's ear. 'You can hear it ticking.'

Still Fleur ignored her. 'Jazz is faster than the others. We all set off together – then it was just him and me.'

Another look of doubt flickered across Mia's face as she tapped the watch. Why wasn't Fleur listening to her? 'It tells us the day and the time – everything.'

Silence from Fleur and that dreamy, faraway look.

Alfie drew Mia away. 'Best to leave her for now,' he whispered as they left the shelter.

151

'Why can't she hear me?' Mia wondered.

'It's the same as before – Fleur's eyes are open but she's dreaming.' At least it was a nice dream this time, not a nightmare, he realized.

As Alfie took out a knife to peel a jackfruit, he did his best to ignore Fleur's ramblings. He concentrated on his task, discarding the leathery green skin and cutting the yellow flesh into chunks that he took back into the shelter. He crouched beside Fleur and gently shook her by the shoulder.

She jerked suddenly and blinked, then stared angrily at him. The rash on her face and arms seemed darker and her lips were cracked and dry. 'What do you want?' she demanded crossly.

Alfie offered her the fruit. 'Go on – have some. It's nice and juicy.'

Fleur turned her head away. 'I don't want any.'

'Drink some water then.'

Mia heard him and brought in a coconut shell cup filled with water.

Alfie slid his arm underneath Fleur's shoulders and raised her up. 'You have to drink,' he insisted.

Reluctantly she took a few sips and then seemed to revive. 'What happened? Was I dreaming?'

'Yep.' Carefully he used his fingertips to brush away the water that dribbled down her chin.

'About swimming with Jazz?'

'Yep.'

Fleur sighed. 'I thought it was real. It felt real!' She could almost taste the salt on her lips and feel the breeze in her hair.

'Never mind. Jazz did actually come to see you, remember?'

'When?' She had a hazy memory of being with the others at the water's edge, of watching Alfie swim with Pearl out to a boat stuck on the rocks, of wishing with all her heart that it had been her and Jazz.

'This morning. I told you the dolphins would come eventually and I was right. Jazz came to say hello.'

Fleur smiled briefly then sighed. 'But we didn't go swimming?'

'No, that was only in the dream.' Alfie realized that his arm had gone numb from propping Fleur up. 'Fetch me one of the *Merlin* life-jackets from that ledge so we can use it as a pillow,' he told Mia.

They got it in place and made Fleur take another drink.

She swallowed and thought for a long time. 'OK – so, before that, was there a storm?'

'Yeah – a tornado. That was real. You were in George's Cave. You said you saw two sailors in a lifeboat and at first we didn't believe you.'

At last the fog seemed to clear and Fleur began to figure out a few things. 'I still wish swimming with Jazz had been real too.'

'It will be,' Alfie promised. 'As soon as you're better.'

'I'm better now,' Fleur decided. She made a feeble effort to sit up properly and swing her legs off the bamboo platform but her head swam and she got double vision. 'Oh,' she groaned as she tried to steady herself.

'Don't stand up,' he warned. 'Here, have another drink.'

'What's wrong with me?' As Fleur sipped, she gazed longingly at the waves lapping the shore.

'You got bitten by an insect.' Alfie didn't bother her

with Rickettsia or any other long names. 'It's given you a fever.'

'But you'll soon be better.' Mia wished she could wave a magic wand. 'Won't she, Alfie?'

'Sure,' he murmured as Fleur emptied the cup then sank back against the makeshift pillow. 'All you have to do now is stay here and rest. Tomorrow you'll be stronger, and the day after that. Before you know it, you won't just be dreaming it – you'll be out in the bay with Jazz for real.'

Seeing that Fleur had closed her eyes, Alfie and Mia quietly backed out of the shaded shelter into the glare of full sunlight. There was no sign of their mum and dad coming back for lunch so they decided on the spur of the moment that they had time to dash back to Echo Cave to fetch the ladder.

'We'd better make it quick,' Alfie said. 'We can't leave Fleur alone for too long.'

Inside the shelter, Fleur lay with her eyes shut listening to their voices. She waited until all was quiet then slowly sat up and fumbled for the yellow lifejacket behind her. It was smooth and cool to her touch.

She lifted it and slipped it over her head, fumbling again with the straps to tie it around her waist. Why were her fingers so clumsy and her head so dizzy? It took her an age to fasten the jacket then stand up and make her way outside.

The glare of the sun blinded her. The beach was dazzling white, bounded by rocky headlands to either side. If she could just get from here to the water's edge, then everything would be all right. Jazz was down there waiting for her. But the sand was scorching hot, the sun blazed down.

She set off, dragging her feet and stumbling, listening to the call of the sea. Jazz would be there. He would swim up and greet her with his high-low whistle, slap his tail against the water as if demanding to know where on earth she'd been.

Alfie's right, she thought. *This time it won't be a dream. This time it will be real.*

Chapter Twelve

Fleur's head was spinning. She reached the shoreline and felt cool water curl around her toes, over her feet, up to her ankles.

The sea sparkled. It stretched on for ever.

She swayed then waded in deeper – up to her knees, feeling the gentle swell of waves. Then up to her waist. The water was crystal-clear, inviting her to go on. She leaned into the next wave and let it lift her free of the soft sand beneath her feet. The life-jacket buoyed her up so there was no need to swim – only turn on her back and float. Staring up into the blue sky, she drifted further out to sea, towards the reef.

When she came close to the rocks, she felt the tug of a cross-current so she turned on to her stomach without noticing that the straps of the life-jacket had worked loose. Her sudden movement allowed it to slip over her head and bob on the surface towards the rocks. Then suddenly it was caught by another current and swept out of reach. Without it, Fleur felt herself sink. The water washed over her head and now she couldn't breathe – she was sinking deeper and deeper until panic set in and she used her arms and legs to push back to the surface. As her head broke clear of the water, she gasped in air then began to kick hard.

The reef was close by, the waves were high and a strong pull of water dragged her towards them. Though she had little strength to carry on kicking, she knew she had to stay clear of the rocks or be dashed against them. *Swim!* she told herself. *Swim!*

As Fleur struggled against the current, Alfie and Mia crested the headland carrying the metal ladder. They walked quickly, eager to get back to the shelter to see how Fleur was doing and only stopping to watch a cormorant swoop down into the water close by. It disappeared head-first with hardly a splash then came up with a silver fish wriggling in its beak.

Alfie followed the big bird's progress. He saw it tilt

back its head and swallow the fish whole. Then he noticed a yellow object floating across the bay. There was no doubt in his mind – it was definitely a life-jacket. He felt a stab of fear – how had it got there?

The life-jacket was being carried out to sea, beyond the reef. He looked again and this time saw a dark head in the water – a swimmer was trying to stay clear of the nearby rocks. It must be Fleur. It couldn't be anyone else. And she was swimming as hard as she could but the current was too strong and it was obvious she wasn't going to make it.

In a flash Alfie knew what he had to do. 'Wait here!' he told Mia, dropping his end of the ladder. He ran to the point of the headland – five strides across rough rock – then took a running dive into the water below. He swam underwater until his lungs were bursting and came up twenty metres out to sea. Then he swam front crawl, arms thrashing, kicking strongly, ploughing ahead faster than he had ever done in his life before.

'Be quick, Alfie!' Mia cried from the headland when she saw what was happening – Fleur still struggling to stay clear of the reef, Alfie swimming to save her.

Fleur's legs had lost all their strength. The pull of the current was too strong and she couldn't fight it. The waves broke over her.

Alfie swam on. He could still see Fleur's head above the water and then he couldn't – she'd vanished. Had she been dragged under or had she been swept out of sight beyond the rocks? 'Hang on – I'm coming!' he yelled. 'Fleur, hang on!'

The waves broke over her in a shower of white spray. She struggled to keep her head above water but she knew she was helpless against the power of the sea.

The roar and crash of breaking waves filled her head. Salt water blinded her.

She heard Alfie's voice yell, 'Hang on!'

She was weak and helpless. It was hopeless.

Three dolphins cut across the bay, their fins slicing through the choppy water. They reached the reef before Alfie then dived down out of sight. They resurfaced and surrounded Fleur – Pearl to her left, Stormy to her right and Jazz in front of her as the waves threatened to fling her against the rocks.

Fleur saw Jazz's face – his mouth open, water

streaming from his domed head, his kind eyes willing her to stay afloat. She reached out.

Alfie swam closer to the reef and felt the pull of the current. As a tall wave rolled towards him, he spotted the dolphins surrounding Fleur. The wave broke in a cloud of white spray. When it cleared, Fleur was holding on to Jazz's flipper and Stormy was beneath her, keeping her afloat. Pearl turned and swam towards him.

He groaned with relief and threw himself at Pearl, flinging his arms around her and hugging her tight.

Pearl held still in his embrace. She waited calmly for him to climb aboard then swam easily to join the others.

'Fleur, you're going to be OK.' Close to, Alfie saw how bad the situation was – she was almost too weak to hold on to Jazz's flipper. 'Can you slide yourself on to his back? Let Stormy lift you – that's cool, he's doing it for you. Now grab Jazz's fin.'

Above the crashing waves Fleur heard Alfie telling her what to do. *Let Stormy lift you, grab Jazz's fin.* The instructions made sense. Before she knew it she lay astride Jazz and the three dolphins had turned away from the reef. Jazz, Stormy and Pearl carried Fleur and Alfie back to shore.

*

'I only wanted to swim with Jazz,' Fleur explained to Katie and James as soon as they arrived.

Once the dolphins had landed them on the beach, Mia had split off from Alfie and Fleur in the entrance to George's Cave and hurried to fetch their mum and dad.

From Lookout Point James had already spotted what was happening out to sea and, with his heart in his mouth, had scrambled down the cliff and reached the beach as Mia had run to meet him. Katie too had heard some shouting and yelling. Guessing something was wrong, she'd rushed back home from Turtle Beach.

Now the whole family was gathered by the seashore.

Katie sat down beside Fleur and put her arms around her. 'It's OK. We know how much the dolphins mean to you,' she said softly.

Fleur rested against her. 'Not just any old dolphin, Mum. It's Jazz who's special – I missed him so much.'

162

'We know you did.' Katie looked up at James. Yes it was foolish, but how could they blame Fleur for doing what she'd done? Or Alfie for risking his life to save his sister?

'I was scared I'd never see him again.'

Alfie squatted down on the other side of Fleur. 'You needn't have worried. He's always there for you. Look right now – out there.' He pointed to Jazz swimming with Pearl and Stormy close to the shore.

'Thanks, Alfie. I just wanted to swim with him,' Fleur said again. 'It was my dream.'

'And we should have listened to you and helped you,' James said. 'We shouldn't have stood in your way.'

'But you were so poorly,' Katie added. 'And the tornado didn't help. We had to make sure you were safe.'

Fleur nodded and looked out to sea. She smiled then waved at Jazz as he turned in the water and slapped his tail against the surface. 'So can I sleep in George's Cave tonight?'

James exchanged doubtful glances with Katie.

'Can I – please?' Fleur's head had started to clear.

Her mum's reasons made sense, but she knew in her heart she'd get better sooner if she could stay closer to Jazz.

'Promise – no midnight swims?' Katie said.

'I promise,' Fleur agreed.

'I'll stay here with her,' Alfie offered. 'We can block the entrance with the insect screen – that way we won't get bitten to death by mozzies.'

Mia jumped in. 'And me. We'll all sleep in the cave.'

'OK, you win,' James decided. 'We'll set you up for a good night's sleep here. But first – you know what I'm going to say?'

'Find firewood?' Mia suggested with a sigh.

'Nope.'

'Collect coconuts? Fetch water?' Alfie grinned.

'No. Guess again.' James watched Katie and Alfie carefully raise Fleur to her feet and support her as they started off up the beach. He overtook them and led the way. 'First, it's time to eat!'

The sun had passed its noonday peak. Stomachs were rumbling. Smoked fish and jackfruit were on the menu.

From the calm waters of the bay, Jazz, Pearl and Stormy watched the family head happily back to camp. They swam in circles, their grey backs gleaming, clicking quietly, making sure that all was well.

*

That night, Fleur, Alfie and Mia fell asleep to the sound of waves lapping the shore.

Fleur's sleep in George's Cave was calm, cool and dreamless. She woke up in the early morning to the whistling call of dolphins. For a while she lay still and listened, staring out through the insect screen at the stars and moon until Alfie and Mia woke too.

Mia was the first to speak. 'Dolphins! Shall we go outside?'

Without saying anything but smiling to himself, Alfie took away the screen. 'See,' he murmured to Fleur as Mia shot out on to the wet sand, 'Jazz is still here.'

Fleur picked out his high-low whistle from Stormy's shrill note and Pearl's chirrup. She stepped outside and raised her hand in greeting.

'How are you feeling?' Alfie asked.

'Better.' She showed him the fading rash on her arms. 'See.'

'But still no swimming,' he reminded her. 'You're not strong enough yet.'

Mia was already splashing in the shallow water, calling out to Stormy and capering along the shoreline. The rising sun cast a pink glow over the bay.

'No swimming,' Fleur promised. 'But I am going to get better now.'

As if he'd heard and understood, Jazz swam close and whacked the surface of the water with his tail flukes. Then he shot back out to sea with a great, show-offy tail-walk that left Pearl and Stormy trailing in his wake.

'I am,' Fleur promised Alfie with a grateful smile.

Their three dolphins leaped clear of the water – once, twice, three times – for the joy of being alive.

'You are,' Alfie agreed.

'Slowly, day by day.' She waded knee-deep into the water and waved both arms above her head. 'Thank you, Jazz. Thank you, Stormy.'

'Thank you, Pearl,' Alfie added.

'And who knows,' Fleur said as she glanced up at the brightening sky to see a thin white trail left by a plane so high in the sky that it could scarcely be seen. 'Maybe those two sailors from *Kestrel* did spot the smoke from our fire.'

'Maybe they did.' Then again, maybe they didn't. Alfie shrugged his shoulders and tried not to let his hopes of rescue rise too high.

Jazz leaped again, rolled in the air then vanished under the water, followed by Pearl and Stormy. They headed for the reef to rejoin their pod and share a breakfast of squid.

'Hungry?' Alfie asked.

'Yep,' Fleur said.

He patted her arm and called for Mia then turned for camp. 'Come on, Mi-mi. Let's eat!'

The story
continues
in ...

Turn the
page for a
sneak peek ...

Chapter One

'Day 27.' Six-year-old Mia Fisher made another notch in the calendar stick.

'That means we've been here for almost four weeks,' her older sister, Fleur, said with a long sigh.

Four weeks marooned on Dolphin Island felt like for ever. Gone from their world were streets and houses, cars and shops. Instead they had sand and palm trees, restless waves and blue skies. And dolphins. Of course – how could Fleur forget about the dolphins? She shook herself then looked eagerly out to sea in the hope of catching sight of Jazz, Stormy and Pearl.

The sun had just risen. Gentle waves lapped at the rocky headlands and the sea sparkled on for ever. But there was no sign of their special dolphin friends.

Mia and Fleur's brother, Alfie, came out of the

shelter carrying the watch that he'd salvaged from the *Kestrel* wreck. The small yacht belonging to two unknown sailors had sunk close to the shore during a recent storm.

Mia took it from him then held it to her ear. Quickly she handed it back. 'Listen to that – it makes a ticking noise.' Her brown hair was tightly braided, her face freckled and tanned.

Alfie grinned. 'That's because it's not digital. It's an old-fashioned watch that you have to wind up,' he explained.

'The kind that Granddad Tony wears,' Fleur added.

A frown appeared on Mia's face. 'I miss him and Gran,' she whispered.

'We all do,' Fleur said sadly. She remembered the last time they'd seen them, standing in the airport to wave them off. That was the day in July when they'd flown out to Australia with their mum and dad then set off from Queensland in their granddad's yacht, *Merlin* – at the start of their big adventure, before the tropical storm that had wrecked their boat and cast them away on Dolphin Island. 'But don't worry – we'll see them again soon.'

'When?' Mia asked.

'When we get rescued.'

'When?'

'Soon.' Fleur gave Mia a quick hug. 'I'll tell you what: who wants to come and look for birds' eggs for breakfast?'

'Me!' Mia jumped at the chance. She skipped and hopped towards the cliff behind the shelter.

'What about you?' Fleur asked Alfie.

'Nope.' He slipped the watch into his pocket then patted the knife tucked inside the waistband of his red swimming shorts. Then he set off across the white sand. 'I'm planning to cut down more bamboo on Turtle Beach.'

The bamboo was for the new raft that their mum and dad had started to build. They wanted to make it stronger and better than the one Alfie had used when he'd set out alone to explore what lay off the southern tip of the island. He'd almost drowned, so this time there would be no going off on solo voyages.

'OK, see you at breakfast.' Fleur had to hurry to catch up with Mia, who was scrambling up the cliff path like one of the monkeys who lived in the forest. She was like a little monkey herself – nimble and surefooted, but easier to spot in her turquoise swimmie. 'Wait for me!' Fleur yelled after her.

Just then their mum, Katie, emerged from the shelter. 'Hats!' she reminded them.

So Fleur had to back-track and grab the two home-made sunhats that her mum presented to her. They were woven out of strips of palm leaf. Mia's first hat had blown away during a hurricane so Fleur had made her a new one, complete with bright red and yellow feathers sticking out of the band that held it together. 'Thanks,' she gasped then raced off up the cliff path.

James Fisher followed Katie out of the shelter. He'd just got up and was rubbing sleep from his eyes. 'Someone's feeling better,' he remarked to his wife as he watched Fleur scale the cliff.

'Yes, thank heavens.' A week earlier their eldest daughter had been laid low with tick-bite fever. She'd been so weak that she hadn't been able to stand and there had been a worry that she might not survive. 'And thanks to Jazz, Pearl and Stormy too.'

Meanwhile, Fleur and Mia carried on up the cliff path. Fleur was glad to be back in action after being so poorly and was, as ever, on the lookout for their friendly dolphins. 'Jazz, where are you?' she said out loud as she paused to look down at the blue water. 'You kept me company while I was sick. Now I want to let you know that I'm better.'

Mia had scrambled on ahead. 'What did you say?' she yelled over her shoulder as a breeze blew strands of hair across her sticky cheeks.

'Nothing. Carry on.'

'Who were you talking to?'

'No one. I said, let's carry on.' *Jazz, where are you?* Fleur thought with another long sigh.

'Fibber!' Mia challenged with a cheeky grin. 'You were talking to Jazz, and he's not even here!'

'OK, I admit it.' Through storm and shipwreck, Jazz, Stormy and Pearl had stayed by the side of the Fisher family. The dolphins had protected them since the day when *Merlin* had sunk – they'd played alongside them and even taught them how to catch fish.

'Hah!' Mia's grin widened. 'You were talking to

Mr Nobody!'

'So?' Fleur said with a shrug. *Come on, Jazz, pay me a visit!* The ocean was calm and completely empty. It was days since they'd spied a passing ship or even a plane flying overhead, and it was only the company of their faithful dolphins that had kept the family going.

'Eggs!' Mia reminded her brightly. 'Come on, slowcoach – I'm hungry!'

Fleur climbed with Mia until they came to Butterfly Falls. Here, she took off her hat and turned it upside down. 'We can store the eggs in here, if we find any,' she suggested.

*

Mia counted eggs as they placed them in the hat. '... Three, four, five. Is that enough?'

'No, that's only one each and gannets' eggs aren't very big.' Fleur decided they had to go on searching the crevices in the rock where the birds laid their eggs. But first she wanted to cool her feet in the stream. She sat on a boulder and dipped them in the clear water, taking time to notice an orange butterfly resting on a broad, shiny leaf that overhung the waterfall.

There were five black spots on each of its brightly coloured wings.

Mia plonked herself down beside Fleur. The startled butterfly took flight. But there was plenty of other nature stuff for Fleur to look at – she spotted three white cockatoos perched in a bush, squawking and making an almighty din, with their yellow crests raised

in anger at the human interruption. Better still, she spied a cane toad squatting on a wet rock at the edge of the waterfall, puffing out his throat and staring back at her with unblinking eyes. Down on the beach there was the usual bird-life; dainty sandpipers waded in the shallow water and black cormorants rested on the rocky headlands, resting between fishing expeditions

far out to sea.

'I'm bored,' Mia said with a loud sigh. 'What can I do?'

'Play the stone tower game,' Fleur suggested. 'See if you can beat your record of fifteen.'

So Mia scrabbled around to find a handful of small, flat stones then she began to balance them, one on top of the other. '... Six, seven, eight.'

'Careful,' Fleur warned as the tower wobbled.

'... Nine, ten, eleven.'

Just then there was a loud squeal from further up the mountain. A startled Mia jerked her hand and the tower of stones toppled.

'Huh!' She stood up and looked angrily up the slope.

Half a dozen macaque monkeys emerged from the forest and sprinted towards them. Two mothers carried babies on their backs, while the big male bared his teeth and led the group to Lookout Point, two hundred metres away from Mia and Fleur. They sat safely upwind of the family's high lookout fire, glancing back up the mountain towards the trees.

'Hmm, I wonder what scared them,' Fleur said,

glancing up towards the edge of the trees. She saw nothing unusual; only dry scrubland and rocks.

'The baby monkeys are so-o-o cute!' Mia left the waterfall and ventured a little way towards them. 'They've got big brown eyes and pointy pink ears. Fleur, come and look.'

Carrying the hatful of eggs with care, Fleur joined her sister on the slope. She loved the macaques even though they sometimes stole down to base camp at night and raided the Fishers' food store. They were a rich brown colour with funny dark tufts of hair on the top of their heads and they got into play-fights where they rolled on the ground and wrestled.

'Aah – one of the mothers is picking nits out of her baby's hair.' Mia crept closer.

'They're not nits, they're parasites.' Fleur smiled at the grooming ritual. Mia was right – the babies were cuter than cute. They were adorable.

'Same thing!'

'Well yes – I guess.' How much nearer could they creep without the macaques running off?

The male in the group watched every step they

made. It looked like he was playing a game of dare – *OK, one more step and another and another, but that's it; no more.* All of a sudden he opened his mouth and let out a high-pitched screech. The whole group leaped from the stone ledge and made a beeline straight for the girls.

'Help, no – shoo, monkeys!' Mia squealed. She grabbed Fleur's arm and dislodged the eggs inside the hat.

'Whoa!' Fleur gave a cry. The eggs fell and smashed on a rock.

In an instant the macaques forgot about the girls and pounced on the broken eggs, scooping up the yolks and cramming them into their mouths. Then they licked their fingers and seemed to grin.

'Huh!' The danger over, Mia sulked and stamped her foot.

'Yummy breakfast for monkeys,' Fleur grumbled. Never mind – that was how life was sometimes on Dolphin Island – frustrating and difficult. 'Come on, Mia. We'll have to start looking all over again.'

*

'Where's Alfie?' James asked as he dished out scrambled eggs and fish fried in coconut oil for a late breakfast.

'He went to Turtle Beach to collect bamboo,' Fleur replied. It had taken ages to search a second time and gather enough eggs for the whole family. Now all she wanted to do was rest and eat.

'Mia, run and find him,' James suggested. 'Tell him I've made a feast fit for a king.'

Mia scooted off down the beach and disappeared over the headland.

'Here – we have to build up your strength.' James presented Fleur with fish and eggs on a plate salvaged from *Kestrel*. 'How are you feeling today?'

'Good,' she told him with her mouth full. 'I'd be even better if Jazz decided to pay me another visit.'

Her dad laughed. 'Yeah, yeah – but remember he has to live his own life and do what dolphins do.'

'Such as?' What could be more fun than swimming with her?

'Catching fish, hanging out with the rest of his pod – breaching, lob-tailing, riding the swell in front of ocean liners – cool stuff like that.'

'I guess.' Fleur wrinkled her nose and stared out to sea.

'You're not sulking, are you?' James checked. Four weeks on the island without shaving meant that his dark beard had grown bushy, his red T-shirt had faded in the sun and the hem on his only pair of shorts had begun to fray.

'No.'

'Not even a little bit?'

'No,' Fleur insisted. The longer she looked, the more certain she was that her dolphin friend was still nowhere to be seen. 'Oh well, I guess I'd better go and collect firewood for Lookout Point.'

'Good girl. Your mum's already up there. Tell her to come down for something to eat.'

As Fleur brushed herself down and got ready to leave camp, Mia reappeared with Alfie. They carried a big bundle of bamboo canes between them, pausing for a rest on the headland before trudging on.

'I'll let Mum know about the new load of bamboo. She'll probably want to get on with building the raft,'

Fleur said.

'You can bet your life she will,' James agreed.

So Fleur took the track up the cliff for the second time that day, picking her way from ledge to ledge until she came to Butterfly Falls. Here she stopped to cup her hands around her mouth and call up to her mum in her loudest voice. 'Mum – more bam-boo! And break-fast!'

Standing by the fire on Lookout Point, Katie heard her and gave her a thumbs-up. She immediately left the ledge and began her descent.

'Hey, Mum. Did you see any dolphins?' Fleur asked as their paths crossed.

'Hey, Fleury.' Katie greeted her daughter then shook her head. 'No. It's unusually quiet out there today, I must say.'

They paused to look out to sea, their hands shading their eyes against the bright sun. The empty horizon seemed to stretch for ever. There was a gentle swell as the white-capped waves met the underwater reef where *Merlin* had met her end.

'The tide's in,' Katie remarked. 'I might go down to

the water's edge in a little while to see if it's brought in anything useful, like old rope or empty bottles.'

'I'm collecting firewood,' Fleur explained. Even though there were no ships on the horizon or planes flying overhead, it was vital to keep both fires fed just in case.

So she said goodbye to her mum then walked on, searching under bushes for twigs and collecting an armful before she reached the lookout. She threw the fuel on the fire then went higher up the mountain in search of bigger branches that had fallen from the trees at the edge of the forest. But the trouble with Fleur was, she was easily thrown off-task. Not like Alfie, who set out to do a thing and saw it through to the end. Like fetching bamboo, for instance – he wouldn't stop hacking at the canes until he'd got enough to build a whole new raft. That was just the way he was. But as for Fleur collecting firewood – well, there were a dozen more interesting things to do.

There was investigating the termite mound at the far side of Lookout Point for a start. How fascinating it was to sit cross-legged on the hillside and watch the teeming columns of white ants go about their mysterious business, marching here and there, here and there. And what about the reddish-brown giant millipede she found attached to the first branch she collected? It was at least twenty centimetres long and deserved a full ten minutes of study. Then there was the crested chameleon sitting on a hot rock, staring at her with his bulbous eyes – not as pretty as George, her pet gecko, but interesting nonetheless.

Best of all, Fleur stood and watched a cloud of small white butterflies flit in the sunlight at the edge of the trees. So pretty. So dainty. She had to tear herself away from them and force herself to enter the shade of the forest, where suddenly the whole world changed.

Instead of light there was deep, dark shadow. If there were creatures in here, they weren't flitting anywhere. They were well hidden behind creepers, under logs or in the treetops. There were no birds singing.

Fleur let her eyes get used to the darkness then she crept forward along a fallen tree trunk, aiming to drag out a hefty branch that had broken off in a high wind. She hoped that this would provide enough wood to keep the fire going for a while. But she had to take care not to fall off the log into the muddy mess of creepers and decaying leaves beneath. That was how she'd picked up the tick that had made her so sick – by stepping into the mud and letting a tick attach itself to her ankle. There were other nasty things living here too. Poisonous snakes for all she knew. And there were definitely rats – she'd seen a big one the last time she was in here.

So she went slowly on all fours until she reached the fallen branch and found that it wasn't too heavy for her to drag it back the way she'd come.

It's Saturday. My friends back home are washing their hair and getting ready to go shopping, she thought ruefully as she heaved at the branch. *They're chatting about music and boys.*

Moving the branch roused a colony of bats in the trees overhead. They were pale creatures with thin, leathery wings that flitted deeper into the forest, away from danger.

It was a struggle, but at last Fleur dragged the dead branch out into the open and down the hillside to the fire. Once there, she wrenched at it and broke off short sections to feed the crackling flames.

'I'll go back into the forest for one more branch like that then I'll take a break,' Fleur said out loud, wiping sweat from her forehead. From her high vantage point she glanced down at the beach.

Alfie and her mum were busy laying out bamboo canes and cutting them all to the same length to build the raft. Mia and her dad played noughts and crosses on giant grids drawn in the sand.

Then Fleur took a long look out to the glittering sea. *Still no dolphins.* She gave a wistful sigh, then slowly and reluctantly made her way back up the mountain and into the forest.

More adventures on
Dolphin Island

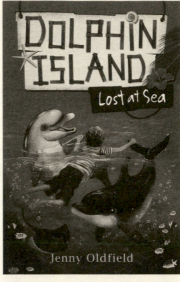

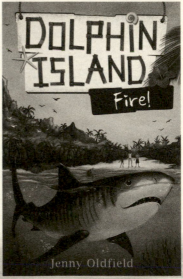

Six books to collect!